What people are say
THE ROSE TATTOO:

UNSPOKEN CONFESSIONS
"The hunt is thrilling, the passion hot, the danger only too real."
—*Affaire de Coeur*

UNLAWFULLY WEDDED
"Extremely well-done."
—*Rendezvous*

UNDYING LAUGHTER
"Already known for her mastery of suspense, Kelsey Roberts displays a glorious sense of humor in UNDYING LAUGHTER...."
—Debbie Richardson, *Romantic Times*

HANDSOME AS SIN
"Kelsey Roberts once again delivers sparkling dialogue and great touches of humor."
—Debbie Richardson, *Romantic Times*

THE TALL, DARK ALIBI
"Ms. Roberts's skillful blending of humor and suspense is once again evident..."
—Debbie Richardson, *Romantic Times*

THE SILENT GROOM
"Kelsey Roberts will take you on a fun, fanciful and fascinating journey... If you are looking for romance and intrigue with a twist, you won't want to miss her."
—Nora Roberts

THE WRONG MAN
"Talented Intrigue author Kelsey Roberts definitely has a way with words and proves it once again."
—Debbie Richardson, *Romantic Times*

Dear Reader,

Her Mother's Arms was truly a labor of love, not for me, but for my editor, Huntley Fitzpatrick, who was *very* pregnant at the time we were working on this book. While I was sorry Huntley went out on maternity leave before seeing the finished product, I was very happy to have my previous editor, Bonnie Crisalli, who worked with me on the creation of THE ROSE TATTOO series, step in at the last minute.

Every now and then, a story seems to write itself and this was one of those stories. I think every author draws on his or her own experiences, and I must admit to using bits and pieces of my own life to give dimension to Hannah and Ian. In this day of blended families, it isn't uncommon to run across a person with some major emotional scars. And often in real life, love doesn't conquer all. Luckily it does in the wonderful world of romance fiction.

I was a fan of the romance genre long before I was lucky enough to publish my first novel. I've always enjoyed the satisfaction of a true happy ending. Ian and Hannah face many challenges and I'll admit Ian was definitely the driving force in this novel. It is always a formidable task to create characters who will experience conflict, yet give them enough in common to make it believable when they live happily ever after in the end. For this book, I didn't have to go much farther than my own backyard. My husband and I have no common interests, a twenty-year gap in our ages and totally different backgrounds. We're approaching sixteen years of happy marriage, so I do believe that opposites can attract and that real love can conquer all. I'm also grateful for our beautiful son, since it's nice to have someone closer to my own age to play with.

Please keep in touch. You can reach me through Connections at Harlequin's web site at www.romance.net.

Warmly,

Kelsey Roberts

Kelsey Roberts

Her Mother's Arms

Harlequin Books

TORONTO • NEW YORK • LONDON
AMSTERDAM • PARIS • SYDNEY • HAMBURG
STOCKHOLM • ATHENS • TOKYO • MILAN
MADRID • WARSAW • BUDAPEST • AUCKLAND

For Huntley and Bonnie,
the best tag team in publishing!

ISBN 0-373-22455-9

HER MOTHER'S ARMS

This edition published by arrangement with Harlequin Books S.A.

Printed in U.S.A.

CAST OF CHARACTERS

Hannah Bailey—All she wanted was the truth—and her real mother's name.

Ian MacPhearson—His CIA background gave him the skills needed to help Hannah. Would the past drive him from her side?

Joleen Hawkins—The quiet waitress spoke little—did she know more?

Gabriel Langston—He hoped his friend Ian would assist a lady in distress.

Joanna Boudreaux Langston—The pregnant attorney needed a break.

Rose Porter—The proprietress of the Rose Tattoo knew she'd never given birth to a baby girl.

Shelby Tanner—The Rose Tattoo's pregnant co-owner always offered solid advice.

Jeffrey Fielding—If all went as planned, the upstanding attorney would soon be a judge.

Colton Mays—When not busy directing the Charleston Society for the Arts, his activities with the Oyster Point Society kept him busy.

Horrace Vanderkemp, MD—As president of the Oyster Point Society, the secretive doctor ran his own agenda.

Dr. Longfellow—He'd delivered Hannah—could he recognize her mother after all this time?

Billy "Skeeter" Pringle—How low would the sleazy car dealer stoop?

Drawing by Linda Harding Shaw

Prologue

"Do you really think she'll show?"

Leaning back against his high-backed leather chair, he quietly regarded his visitor as he pondered the question. "I think Miss Hannah Bailey poses a real threat, don't you?"

His visitor began to squirm in the seat as small beads of perspiration formed on his brow and upper lip. "I don't think she can find anything. Not after all this time."

"Have you been able to determine which child she is?"

He shook his head. "Not yet, but I have it narrowed down to three or four probables."

"Probables?" he repeated softly. "I paid you well to make certain nothing like this ever happened."

"I know, I know," the man babbled.

He hated babbling. It was so weak.

"When will you know if she has, in fact, made good on her threats to come to Charleston?"

"I sent a man to New Orleans to keep an eye on her. He's been there a week already."

"I have a copy of her letter," he said as he patiently unfolded the crisp, white document and passed it across his desk. "It would appear that Miss Bailey has contacted every social services agency and every courthouse in the state looking for answers."

"It won't matter. Even if she does manage to get something, the records were doctored even before they were filed. She can't trace anything back to us."

"Us?" He rose, sighing deeply as he did. "There is no *us*. There hasn't been for nearly twenty years. I'm in no position to have the past come back to haunt me now. Do you understand?"

The man's face flushed with anger, but he knew better than to go on the offensive. "What do you want me to do?"

"I want you to stay away from me. I can't have you dropping in on me."

"What am I supposed to do if she comes snooping around here?"

"If Miss Bailey is so determined to climb her family tree, it would seem only fitting that she meet the same fate as the others."

The man's flush drained until his face was nearly as white as his shirt. "You want me to kill her?"

Chapter One

"I see you still wear your hair like a girl," Ian said as he gave his friend a smart slap on the back before yanking his dark ponytail.

Gabe Langston offered a half smile along with his hand, then motioned Ian to the seat next to his.

Ian MacPhearson gave his unfamiliar surroundings a pretty thorough once-over as he joined his longtime friend and his wife, Joanna, at the polished round table near glass doors that led to a porch beyond. The Rose Tattoo restaurant wasn't exactly what he had envisioned from Gabe's letters. On the other hand, Gabe's new bride was everything he had said she was. A fiery redhead with devotion for her husband clearly visible in her blue eyes.

"Nice to finally meet you," Joanna said. Her hand rested on her belly, swelled from the early state of her pregnancy. Her other hand was draped affectionately over Gabe's shoulder.

"Will I be labeled a pig if I say you are as beautiful as Gabe said?" Ian asked.

Joanna's blush was faint, but a warm, appreciative smile reached her eyes. "Not as long as it comes from a friend of Gabe's."

Ian crossed his booted leg, gripping his ankle as he settled against the wooden chair. From his vantage point, he could watch the flurry of activity that seemed to emanate from twin chrome doors with porthole-shaped windows. Each time one of the doors opened, the room filled with mouthwatering aromas. His stomach growled as if he needed a reminder that he hadn't eaten since leaving his secluded Montana home ten hours earlier.

"I'm famished," Joanna exclaimed.

Gabe gave a theatrical sigh as his hazel eyes rolled. "When *aren't* you famished?" he teased.

Ian felt a mild stab of jealous heartache as he silently watched the couple. Had Carmen really been gone for five years?

"Cut her a break, Langston. She's eating for two." Ian looked around the room, counted no fewer than four pregnant ladies and said, "Being with child seems to be a popular theme in these parts."

Joanna nodded. "I warned Gabe that there had to be something in the water here. Just a few months ago, Tory had a little girl."

"Tory?" Ian asked.

"Gabe's sister-in-law."

Ian was about to ask for further details, when a tall, willowy woman with big green eyes, hair the color of a brilliant red Christmas tree skirt and a big silver stud protruding from her nostril approached. He noticed two distinct things when she arrived—first, her odd appearance didn't seem to faze Gabe or his wife; second, she smelled rather medicinal.

"Welcome!" she exclaimed with her pad poised. "I'm Susan, and Gabe has told us all about you. I'll be your waitress. I'd be really happy if you would ask for me the next time you came in."

Joanna cleared her throat. "You'll have to excuse Susan," she said. "I think the formaldehyde is killing off what few brain cells she had in the first place."

The comment was made without malice and it seemed to have no effect on the waitress. In fact, she proudly twirled around, allowing her lace-and-satin dress to billow out from around her legs. It also intensified the scent of embalming fluid. "That wasn't a come-on," Susan insisted. "I just need to hustle tips so I can buy some more of these dresses. I love this look," she gushed. "Rose is furious but she can't really say anything, since I agreed to cover for Joleen tonight."

"Rose is your..."

"Her boss, my mother," Gabe finished. "She should be back in a few minutes. She had to run to the bank. She's dying to meet you."

"And I'm in a bit of a hurry to take your orders," Susan said. "The chef is on another rampage, so we'd better get moving before he decides to quit."

Since he was unfamiliar with the offerings of the Charleston restaurant, he ordered last, selecting a broiled fish entrée. Gabe selected a bottle of wine, then sent Susan scurrying on her way.

"Want to explain the formaldehyde?" Ian asked.

Joanna and Gabe shook their heads in unison. "Susan Taylor is a very strange woman," Gabe said.

"Strange, but sweet," Joanna interjected. "Her latest fixation is coffin chic."

Ian raked his hand through his hair. "Coffin chic?"

Joanna leaned as close as her swollen body would allow, then rested her elbows against the table. "Some woman down on Market Street opened a dress shop that specializes in clothing made from the remnants of the materials used to make the linings in coffins. She claims that by wearing those things, you can get in touch with the next world."

"Well, it fits," Ian said with a sigh. "Susan certainly seems like she's in another world."

"She's really harmless," Gabe insisted. "But I didn't invite you here to discuss the waitress's eclectic fashion sense."

Ian watched as Joanna reached out and gave her husband's hand a warning squeeze. "Dinner first," she said as a reminder.

Gabe shrugged. "She's right. So, what have you been up to?" he asked when the bottle of wine arrived.

It was Ian's turn to shrug. "Keeping busy."

"How can cows keep you busy?" Gabe asked. "What do they do besides eat and moo?"

Ian laughed. "City boy. A ranch is a lot of work."

Gabe poured Ian a generous amount of Chablis. "And you have enough money to pay people to do that work for you."

"I'd go nuts sitting around doing nothing other than writing checks all day."

Joanna chuckled. "I wouldn't mind giving it a whirl."

"Anytime you want to retire, go for it," Gabe said, as if it wasn't the first time the subject had been broached by the couple.

"Is tending cattle fulfilling?"

Joanna's question caught him off guard. He hadn't thought about his life in terms of fulfilling or useful for years. "It keeps me busy."

"That's no way to live," she chided softly. "Gabe told me you were a great agent when you were with the CIA. How can you go from all those adrenaline rushes to sitting on a porch at your secluded hideaway? Gabe showed me some pictures of your place." Joanna took a sip of water. "Is it true that the easiest way to get to your ranch is by private airplane? You must feel like you're marooned on a deserted island."

"I like my privacy," Ian said. "No neighbors for miles. Unless you count the Baylor place, but that's a good ten miles away."

"No one to talk to," Joanna countered. "That would make me loony."

Gabe draped his arm around his wife's shoulder. "Joanna is your exact opposite. You've slowed down to a stop, she's stuck in high gear."

"I am not," Joanna huffed. "I've just got responsibilities."

"Do you like practicing law?" Ian asked, hoping to steer the conversation away from Gabe's apparent disapproval of her choice to attempt the difficult juggling act of career and family.

Joanna's whole body seemed to come alive at the question. Her broad smile reached all the way to her eyes. "I just recently was reminded why I got into it in the first place."

"You defended Rose, right?" Ian asked.

"Beautifully," Gabe answered, then gave his wife a kiss on the forehead. "She's Charleston's version of Perry Mason. She even uncovered the real murderer just before they rolled the final credits."

"Impressive," Ian said with a nod of acknowledgment and a lift of his wineglass.

"She'd be a hell of a lot more impressive if she'd follow her doctor's advice and take some time off."

Ian turned in the direction of the boisterous voice. The woman was short, made taller by a pair of gravity-defying spiked heels that clicked rhythmically as she crossed the wooden floor. He guessed her age to be somewhere in the fifties, though she apparently went to great lengths to challenge the truth of her years. Her hair was platinum, teased into a style that immediately reminded Ian of old photographs of a blond Gladys Presley. Maybe that was just because Elvis tunes had been playing on the jukebox nonstop since he arrived. She had to be Gabe's long-lost biological mother. Gabe was also an Elvis freak.

Without disturbing a single hair on her head, Rose bent down and kissed the cheeks of Gabe and Joanna in turn. Then she gave Ian a long, searching look. "So, Mr. MacPhearson, you finally answered Gabe's call for help."

Ian felt perplexed. There had been nothing urgent about Gabe's letters, nothing that had given him the impression that his good friend was up to anything other than enjoying his recent marriage, happily anticipating the birth of their first child and simply wanting him to come and see for himself. At least, that was what he had said. Ian now suspected there was more to it than that.

Gabe's expression was a little guilty, while Joanna offered her mother-in-law a rather stern look. "We were waiting until after dinner," she explained. "We thought Ian would be helpless to refuse if he mixed jet lag with a gourmet meal."

Rose simply sighed as if it didn't matter that she had foiled the as-yet-to-be-explained secret. She sat in the empty chair to Ian's left, adjusting a wide patent-leather belt that cinched the waistband of her leopard-print stretch pants. He noted that in spite of the heavy makeup and gaudy costume jewelry, Rose Porter didn't look cheap. In a strange sort of way, she exuded a confidence, as if her taste—or lack thereof—was her way of telling any and all that she was quite comfortable with who and what she was. She didn't seem to care about convention and he found that instantly appealing.

"Sorry to spoil your fun," Rose began, "but I'm more concerned with Joanna's health. I've got enough to worry about with Kendall just weeks away from delivering her baby, and Shelby can barely come into work anymore thanks to morning sickness."

Ian smiled at Joanna. "Is there some sort of baby boom here in Charleston? I'm beginning to understand your comment about the water possibly being tainted with fertility drugs here."

Rose scoffed. "Water my foot. My family is just passionate by nature."

"Who are Kendall and Shelby?" Ian asked.

Rose motioned to the bartender, who produced a mug of steaming coffee almost instantly. "Kendall is my niece. She and her wacky husband, Jonas, have another month to go. Shelby is my partner. She's already got a beautiful three-year-old little boy—"

"Beautifully spoiled," Gabe injected. "He's a great kid, but no one has ever uttered the word *no* to Chad."

Rose gave her son a well-meaning swat on the arm. "Shelby also has the most precious daughter, Cassidy. She's the spitting image of her father. She'll break a lot of hearts down the road."

Ian gave an exaggerated leer. "Maybe I should plan a return trip when she's of age."

"You'd have to get past Dylan," Gabe warned. "He's ATF and, like Shelby and my mother, they'd kill anyone who even so much as looked funny at any of their kids again."

"Can you blame them?" Joanna asked. Her

hand went protectively to her belly. "I don't know what I would do if anyone ever threatened this little guy."

Visions of terrible things happening to someone he had loved flashed painfully through Ian's mind. "Someone threatened their children?" Ian asked.

"Child—Chad. But it was a long time ago," Rose answered. "Chad was kidnapped, but it all worked out in the end."

Some of the tension ebbed from Ian's body. "With so many expectant moms, it sounds like you might have to start adding strained foods to the menu here," he teased.

Rose stroked her chin. "Maybe that isn't such a bad idea. Very trendy. I'd have lots of clients. Shelby, Kendall, and you haven't even met Haley yet. She's got another three months. Then there's my other daughter-in-law, Destiny Talbott—"

"*The* Destiny Talbott? The comedienne?" Ian choked out in surprise.

"Right the first time." Rose laughed. "Only if my son Wesley has anything to say about it, Destiny will be planning a nursery next year instead of tour dates."

"Sounds like you have a nice family, Rose," Ian said.

"What you need is a nice girl—"

"Rose!" Gabe cut in forcefully.

While Ian was grateful to his friend for saving him from the well-intentioned sentiment that always followed the "nice girl," he was too tired to go into the rather sordid details of his past. It was easier not to think about what he had done.

"Sorry," Rose grumbled. Cradling the mug of coffee between her palms, she turned and quietly studied Ian. There was something wise, yet almost sad, about the way she was looking at him.

"No problem," he said, hoping to lighten the mood. "Gabe tells me you've got one of the hottest places in Charleston here."

Rose's smile was genuine. "*The* hottest," she corrected, "but it belongs to Shelby and me. She figures out what needs to be done and I do it."

As Rose tilted her head, parrot-shaped earrings danced against her lobes. The exotic bird motif was repeated in her necklace and again on an appliqué on the front of her snug-fitting black shirt. Rose Porter was the exact opposite of Ester Langston, Gabe's adoptive mother. He had known his neighbors, the Langstons, well while growing up, and he guessed the closest Ester had ever gotten to a parrot was on a trip to her private villa on the Mexican Riviera.

"The location has a lot to do with it," Rose explained. "And the tourists love seeing a *real* Charleston single house, complete with dependency."

"Dependency?" Ian asked.

"Summer kitchen and servants' quarters." Rose stood, taking his hand in the process. "If you're going to be here awhile, I'll give you a tour."

"Awhile?" Ian asked, but his question was pointedly ignored.

Instead, Joanna called out, "But our dinner!"

"He's been on a plane for hours," Rose yelled

over her shoulder. "We'll be back long before that useless excuse for a chef gets entrées on the table. You all are the last meals for the night, hopefully that fool can manage to prepare them right."

"You don't like your chef?"

"He can't make decent hopping John," Rose answered, as if that said it all.

At Ian's blank look she added, "hopping John is a traditional Southern staple. You ought to try it."

Ian was led past the horseshoe-shaped bar, through the double doors, into the kitchen. Steam swirled up toward massive ceiling fans as a portly man in an impeccably crisp, white uniform stood at a counter, using a paring knife like an artist's tool as he formed a rose out of the skin of a tomato. Ian noted that the man failed to look up from his task even when Rose uttered introductions.

"I hear you already met the walking dead," Rose grumbled as she glared at Susan, who was stacking dishes in an industrial dishwasher.

"Susan said hello," Ian answered before erasing the hurt from Susan's eyes with a playful wink.

Following Rose, Ian found himself climbing a narrow set of stairs to a second floor. The wooden planks creaked beneath his weight, and he had to duck, the low ceiling hinting that the house had probably been constructed prior to the Civil War, when few men topped the six-foot mark.

Rose continued to grumble. "If I didn't need a

new chef who I'll have to break in, I'd probably fire Susan the Strange tomorrow."

"She seems friendly enough."

Pivoting on the top landing, Rose turned so that they were eye level. "She's wearing dead people's clothes," she argued. "Before that it was Feng Shui, crystals, mediums, pyramids and channeling."

Ian bit back a smile. "I thought her dress was made from the remnants of the fabric they use to line coffins." He smiled. "If it makes it easier, try to think of it as a form of recycling."

Uttering a rather colorful expletive, Rose turned and walked to the end of the hallway. "You can call it recycling, I call it sick. But then, with Susan, I shouldn't have been the least bit surprised."

The office was one large room with two distinct areas. One was slightly cluttered, the other was completely feminine. Rose shoved a stack of catalogs off a chair on the cluttered side. Apparently, Shelby was the Felix Unger of this duo. "Sit so we can get acquainted."

"Won't Gabe and Joanna think—"

She waved her hand in a quieting gesture. "The only thing Gabe thinks about is Joanna."

The seat was soft and did wonders for the stiffness in his back courtesy of his long, cramped flight. "I'm glad to see him happy."

Rose's face was the very picture of maternal pride. "He's a wonderful man. The Langstons did a great job with him."

Ian agreed. "He wasn't the easiest kid to handle."

Perched on the edge of her desk, Rose eyed him with renewed interest. "I thought you and Gabe became friends working on some case back when he was an officer in New York."

Ian nodded, then laced his fingers and cradled the back of his head. "We grew up in the same section of Manhattan. We went to the same schools, but I was a year or two ahead of him. It wasn't until we worked on a drug case about seven years ago that we really got to know each other."

"He said you quit the CIA?"

"True," Ian answered as he schooled his expression to remain bland.

Rose pursed her lips, giving him the impression that she wasn't at all used to evasion. Too bad. He didn't discuss his past with anyone, including his own guilty conscience.

Rose frowned before slipping off the desk, moving behind it and taking her seat. "I was kind of hoping you owed my son a favor."

"A favor?"

Tapping her highly polished pink nails on the desktop, Rose let out a slow breath. "Yeah, like maybe you and Gabe were pinned down in some alley, gunshots ricocheting everywhere," she said as dramatically as any Academy Award winner. "You're hit in the chest and in danger of being hit again, and my son drags you to safety just before you die from your wound."

Ian laughed. "Sorry, Mrs. Porter."

"Rose."

"Sorry, Rose, but the most dangerous thing Gabe and I ever did while we were on a case had more to do with shots of Jack Black than gunfire."

"Too bad," Rose mused. "I was hoping."

"For what?"

Muffled footfalls hurried from the stairs, growing louder and more determined by the second.

"Hey, lady! You can't go up there!" Ian recognized Susan's frazzled voice.

He turned his head and stood in one motion, sensing trouble. It wasn't so much the panicked sound of Susan's voice, but simple instinct.

Perfection was the word that sprang to mind the instant she burst, breathlessly, into the room. Her eyes were wide, a blend of fierce resolve and determination. Their color was also an amalgam, a sensual mixture of clear blue highlighted with shimmering silver rings. They reminded him of a flash of light captured by time-stop photography. They had to be those cosmetic contact lenses. No one had eyes that color naturally.

And while he was on the topic of natural, one lightning-fast glance at her body made him wonder which parts were the work of nature and which were the expertise of some high-priced plastic surgeon. He didn't think the good Lord made bodies that perfect.

"Are you Rose Porter?" the blonde demanded as she stopped abruptly in the doorway.

Ian saw Susan skid to a stop behind the blonde, followed almost immediately by Gabe.

Training tensed his body, coiling him in preparation for the unknown.

Rather leisurely, Rose stood, patted her lacquered hair and offered the intruder a reproachful glare. "Who are you? And what do you think you're doing barging up here?"

Apparently undeterred, the woman entered the office. A slightly rumpled manila folder was clasped in her long, tapered fingers. As she moved, Ian noticed three things. First, she was petite but perfectly proportioned. Secondly, golden highlights from the overhead light shimmered off her shoulder-length hair, giving it the kind of silky softness that fairly dared a man to reach out and touch it. Lastly, he noticed that she was one of those women who could make a simple pair of jeans and a red cotton sweater look like haute couture.

She took another step inside the room. The faint scent of gardenia came with her. "Are you Rose Porter?" she asked again.

Rose shrugged and said, "Yes. So who are you?"

By the time she had finished her question, Gabe had slipped past the blonde and was now at Ian's side. Gabe also seemed to sense that something was wrong.

"My name is Hannah Bailey."

If that was supposed to work as an explanation, it fell a little short. Rose showed no reaction and one brief look at Gabe told Ian that his friend was equally clueless.

"Go back downstairs," Rose told Susan, who

wasted no time following the directive as she uttered something about bad auras under her breath.

"Now," Rose continued as she turned her green eyes on the blonde. "If you're selling something, Shelby handles all that and she isn't here in the evenings. I suggest you—"

"I'm not selling anything and I don't care who Shelby is. I came to see you."

In spite of the force and confidence he heard in the blonde's voice, Ian also noticed a slight tremor in her hands.

"You've seen me," Rose answered abruptly. "You've also interrupted me. Unless this is urgent, I suggest you come back another time—after you make an appointment. Goodbye, Miss Bailey, you're keeping me from dinner with my family."

"Really?" the blonde asked in a tone that dripped with hostility. "Then maybe I should join you."

Rose snorted. "You're a pushy one," she said. "The restaurant is no longer serving dinner. I'm in the middle of a private family gathering, and you are starting to get on my last nerve."

Ignoring the veiled threat, the blonde tossed the envelope on Rose's desk and said, "Once you see what's in there, I think you'll be happy to invite me to stay."

"I'll invite the police if you aren't out of here in the next minute," Rose said as she tossed the envelope back at the woman.

The blonde smiled without humor. "But you said you were having dinner with your family."

"Well, at least that proves you aren't hard-of-hearing." Rose sneered.

"I'm not hard of hearing," Hannah agreed. "I'm your daughter."

Chapter Two

To their credit and much to the chagrin of the chef, Hannah was offered dinner, which she politely declined. When the others finished their meals, Rose suggested that Hannah give them some privacy and she was shown to the porch. For more than an hour Hannah found herself seated at a large table on the side porch of the Rose Tattoo with her as yet still unopened envelope in her lap.

The way Charleston was designed, the houses all stood at angles, apparently to catch the cool air. Though they appeared small from the street, the lots were deep; some even had stunning gardens. The house across the alley from the Rose Tattoo had a beautiful garden, a kind of secret surprise she hadn't expected. It caused Hannah to experience flashes of what she had always called the Garden Trips of her childhood. Shaking her head, she dismissed those memories.

When the dining room was empty of paying guests, the chef and the other employees finished their duties and left. The front door was now locked, making her feel very much like a prisoner of war.

And it sure felt like war. The battle lines had been drawn almost the instant she had made her announcement. "Blast," she muttered under her breath.

"I'd have picked another word."

Lifting her head, she watched as the tall, dark-haired man came through the glass double doors carrying two tumblers of amber liquid. He had been part of the contingent that had huddled in the small second-floor office after dinner. He was the one they called Ian. Hannah mused that it had been a pretty tight squeeze. Both men were well over six feet, but this one wore snakeskin boots that probably added an additional two or three inches. As she watched him come toward her, she wondered what his relationship was to Rose Porter. Though he had the same midnight black hair as Gabe, his eyes were grayish blue rather than hazel. Since they weren't the same blue as her own, Hannah was left to wonder how many children Rose might have conceived with how many different men.

"I thought you could use this," he said as he offered her a drink before joining her at the rectangular table.

"Thanks." She sipped the strong drink, allowing it to burn her throat with the hope that it might replace the burn of tension in her stomach. This wasn't turning out at all as she had planned. "Are we cousins? Half siblings, what?" she asked as she met his intense gaze.

His smile was lazy and just sensual enough to make her feel things that would be offensive to God and nature if they were related somehow.

He chuckled. "Sorry, I'm just a friend of Gabe's. Ian MacPhearson," he added as he extended a dark, deeply tanned hand.

His hand engulfed her own. His eyes never left hers as the contact lasted just a fraction of a second longer than it should have. Hannah wasn't sure whether he was offering basic friendship or pity and, until she was sure, she backed away, leaning against her chair as he took the seat next to her. Ian, apparently, was partial to generic jeans and expensive golf shirts. The silver shirt complemented his midnight black hair and brought out the gray in his eyes. It was a deadly combination, one she would do well to ignore. But as he sat down, he was close enough for her to catch the scent of soap that seemed to cling to his body. And what a body it was. He had the look of a well-conditioned athlete. He wasn't muscle-bound, but she doubted he had more than half a percent of body fat—and that included his earlobes!

Sounds of traffic and muffled voices wafted through the alley on the warm breeze coming off the harbor. The soothing feel of the air wasn't enough to ease the very real sense of turmoil that had her feeling anxious and impatient.

"Drink up," Ian suggested. "I've always found alcohol—in moderation—goes a long way toward making a tough task bearable."

While nervously pushing strands of her straight

hair behind her ear, Hannah used her free hand to take another sip. All the while, she watched her companion. "So, who are you, and why did you get sent out to the porch to deal with me?"

That made him smile. But it was so much more than just a smile. It was a warm, disarming gesture that caused a tingling flutter in her stomach. *Must be the Scotch.*

He rubbed his eyes and stifled a yawn. "I came to visit Joanna and Gabe. At this particular time, I'm down here because I had the distinct impression that Rose wanted to talk to her family in private."

Hannah felt herself tense at the mention of the word *family.* "This wasn't how I had planned to tell her."

Ian's expression gave away nothing of his thoughts. "What was your plan?"

Hannah shrugged, then finished her drink. A few seconds later, she was feeling more relaxed. For that, she silently thanked the man. "I had envisioned something more along the lines of 'Hi, I'm Hannah, your long-lost daughter. I've come from New Orleans to meet you.' Guess I blew that, huh?"

Ian cocked his head to the side and gave her a halfhearted smile. "Your delivery did fall a bit short of tactful."

"Nerves," she admitted. "I tend to talk first and think second when I'm flustered. Which is why I made such a lousy litigator."

Ian's smile vanished. "You're an attorney?"

Nodding, she answered, "Technically. I work

for one of those two-hundred-plus-partner firms in New Orleans. I write and research appellate briefs."

She noted that his angled features had grown as hard as granite. "Using the Constitution to put scum back on the street?"

Hannah flinched at the subtle hostility behind his words. "That *is* the purpose of the Constitution," she explained stiffly. "Or are you one of those people who thinks the Constitution should only be applied when it conforms to public opinion?"

Ian downed the last of his drink. "I think the founding fathers couldn't have anticipated drug lords, terrorists, serial killers and repeat offenders." He punctuated the remark by leaving long enough to return with a half-full bottle.

Hannah politely covered her empty glass with her hand. He poured himself what appeared to be a double.

"The system only works when the rights of the worst of society are protected. Then we can be sure the rights of the innocent will be protected."

Ian uttered a rather colorful curse. "Spoken like a woman who has never been in the trenches. Spend a little time with some career criminals and you'd probably change your tune in a New York minute."

"Is this personal for you? Or are you just anti-lawyer?"

Ian's gaze dropped to his glass. "I'm anti anything that allows criminals to go unpunished."

"Are you a cop?"

"Used to be. I was Agency," he said as he took a long swallow. "Now I lead a very quiet, very calm life on my ranch in Montana."

Hannah was genuinely surprised. "CIA?"

He nodded.

"You were one of those guys that our government trains to circumvent the law and kill people with a strand of your own hair?"

His laugh was deep and rich. A sound that seemed to snap the wire of tension that had stretched between them.

"We did what was necessary to maintain national security."

It was Hannah's turn to laugh. "That's as sanitized as that wonderful expression 'preemptive strike.' Preemptive strike is bombing something, not preempting anything."

Pushing the bottle into the center of the table, she saw Ian eye her manila folder. "What's in there?"

"Proof," she answered simply. When he reached for it, she snatched it out of his grasp. "I think Rose should be the first to see it. Realizing I have some of these things will probably come as big a shock to her, as it was to me."

His dark brows drew together in a questioning arch. "Shock?"

Hannah never had an opportunity to answer. Rose, followed by Joanna and Gabe, arrived, looking a little less hostile than when they had told her to wait on the porch. Still, they didn't exactly look as if they were ready to welcome her with open arms.

Gabe arranged chairs so that Hannah remained seated on one side of the table next to Ian, still clutching her envelope. Gabe and Joanna were on the opposite side. Rose took the seat at the head of the table, placing a sizable brown document file in front of her.

Rose was looking at Hannah with a bland expression. At least the anger seemed to have dissipated.

"Should I excuse myself?" Ian asked as he half rose.

Gabe grabbed his arm and said, "No. You might be needed."

Hannah leaned over to Ian and whispered, "In case they want you to kill me and dispose of my body."

"What?" Joanna and Gabe asked in unison.

"Joke," Ian said. "I was telling Hannah about my previous life."

Gabe's expression could only be described as startled. "All of it?"

Ian just gave his friend one of those leave-it-alone looks. Hannah's innate curiosity was piqued, but she didn't think this the time nor the place to delve into Ian's secrets.

"Miss Bailey," Rose began.

"Don't you think Hannah is more appropriate under the circumstances?" she corrected.

Rose sucked in a breath and let it out audibly. "Hannah," she started again, "there has to be some misunderstanding. I am not your mother." Her green eyes softened. "Not that I wouldn't have loved to have had a daughter."

"You did," Hannah insisted. "In 1967 at the Charleston Girls' Home." Her statement seemed to get the attention of Gabe and Joanna.

"I'm afraid that isn't possible. I was married to Joe Don Porter in 1958. I had J.D. in 1959 and Wesley in 1962. There was no reason for me to have a baby—especially not a daughter—and then give her away."

"No reason except that you divorced in 1963," Hannah supplied as she opened her envelope and dramatically extracted one of the items. Carefully, she unfolded the slightly yellowed newspaper clipping. Beneath the full-color photograph was a caption identifying Rose and her employees; friends and supporters all stood in front of the Rose Tattoo. There was a detailed article about Rose's arrest and the subsequent dismissal of the murder charges nearly a year earlier. Scanning the small print, Hannah found the portion she sought. "'...Mrs. Porter and the victim underwent a nasty divorce in 1963, culminating in Mrs. Porter losing custody of her two young sons.'" Hannah looked up to see pain in Rose's eyes, and she felt a stab of guilt at having caused it. "You weren't married to Mr. Porter when you had me," Hannah said. "But I want you to know up front, I came here to meet you. Maybe develop a relationship. I don't want anything from you—" she paused and took a fortifying breath "—except the name of my biological father."

"I did lose custody of my boys, but I was so busy working my tail off to get them back from Joe Don and the Coed that I didn't have time for a date, let alone to do what is required to get pregnant."

"Hannah, Rose isn't your mother." The statement came from Gabe.

She turned her eyes on him. "How can you know that?"

"Because Rose did have a baby at the Charleston Girls' Home—but that was in 1957, and I'm that baby."

Rose started to reach for Hannah's hand but stopped in mid-action. "Putting Gabe up for adoption almost killed me, even though I know it was what was best for him at the time," Rose explained. "But you have to understand, I was seventeen and stupid. I could *never* have done it again."

Hannah blinked and felt her mind swirl. Ian must have sensed the effect of this unexpected twist, because she felt his callused palm cover her hand. She looked from Rose to Gabe and tried to reconcile what her investigation back in New Orleans had uncovered with what she had just been told.

"But it isn't just the article," Hannah argued, reaching back into her envelope. "I have a copy of my birth certificate. It *says* you're my mother."

Rose reviewed the certificate first, then Gabe. Finally, Joanna did likewise.

Joanna was the first to offer an opinion. "Do you know Dr. Longfellow?" she asked Rose. "He was the OB."

"I've never heard that name before in my life," Rose insisted. "Gabe?"

"The state of New York issued a new birth certificate for me when the Langstons adopted me."

"This is all very interesting," Hannah interjected, "but nothing I've heard explains why my mother kept all these things. Or why we came to Charleston every summer until I was five."

"Maybe your family liked Charleston," Rose suggested.

"Or, you *are* my mother, just like my birth certificate says. This must have been the only way my adoptive mother could think of to tell me the truth."

"What?" Ian gasped. "She just now told you that you were adopted?"

Removing the final item from the envelope, Hannah was careful to keep it hidden in her hand. "I didn't find out until after they died," she explained. "They were killed about three months ago in a car accident in New Orleans."

"Is that where you live?" Joanna asked.

"I've lived my whole life in New Orleans. My parents were wonderful and I really miss them, which is why it was so surprising to learn they had kept this from me for thirty-one years."

"Or, you were adopted in New Orleans and this stuff had some other meaning to your mother," Ian said. When Hannah gave him a disgusted look, he amended, "Except for the birth certificate."

"I checked all over the state of Louisiana. I wasn't adopted there and, according to all the officials I showed this birth certificate to, they insist I was adopted in Charleston."

"Learning all this so soon after losing your parents must have come as a real shock," Ian offered with genuine sympathy in his tone.

Hannah looked at Joanna and noted definite signs of fatigue around her eyes. Her guilt was mounting by the second. From what little she had picked up, Joanna's pregnancy wasn't an easy one, and involving her in this tangled mess probably wasn't the best idea.

"It did," Hannah agreed. "Just like this is a shock for you, Joanna. Maybe Gabe should take you home to rest. You don't look too well."

"She's right," Gabe said, gently pulling his wife into an embrace. "We'd best call it a night."

"Please! Just a little longer," Rose said. "I've got an idea."

"That's trouble," Gabe muttered, which earned him a stern look from his mother.

"Hear me out," Rose chided her son. "All she has is a phony birth certificate. You're a private investigator and Joanna is a lawyer, surely you can help her find the truth."

"Will the truth include this?" Hannah asked as she thrust her hand forward, revealing the small item in her palm.

Gabe took the item and examined it for a minute. "It's a lapel pin from the Oyster Point Society."

"How does this pin prove that I'm supposed to be your mother?" Rose asked. "Oyster Point is a men's-only club. How can you think this bolsters your claim that I'm your mother?"

"I've decided it must have belonged to my father," Hannah explained. "He probably gave it to you as a keepsake, then you gave it to me before you placed me for adoption. Something that would bond us together."

"I'm truly sorry, Hannah, but we aren't bonded. Not by that pin and not by blood. I think I would remember if I'd given birth."

Rose's face contorted as if deep in thought. "The men that belong to Oyster Point wouldn't have given a girl like me the time of day. Remember, in 1966 I had two toddlers I was fighting to get back. I was working day and night tending bar and waiting tables. I even pumped gas one summer for extra cash. Besides, those lapel pins are like wedding bands to those hoity-toity fools. They wouldn't just give one away." Rose reached for Hannah again, this time patting the back of her hand. "I promise you, Hannah, I am *not* your mother."

"Then why did my mother save the pin and the birth certificate in a shoe box in her closet? And why would she have that picture of you taken less than a year ago stashed in with the other things?"

"How should I know?" Rose answered. "But I do honestly feel for you. I'm also not real thrilled that someone put my name on a birth certificate. Gabe will get to the bottom of this and Joanna can do whatever legal stuff needs to be done to get you a correct birth certificate, and maybe we can find your biological parents."

"Hang on," Gabe fairly yelled. "As much as I sympathize, Hannah, we can't help you."

"Why can't we?" Joanna asked.

Gabe reached into his jacket pocket and pulled out a small folder. "Remember?" he prompted his wife by waving what looked like plane tickets. "We were going to ask Ian to take over for me so that we could get away for a while."

Joanna pouted slightly. "But—"

"No buts," Gabe interrupted. "We agreed that we would take your doctor's advice and get away for a while."

"What about me?" Ian asked. "Ever think of sharing this plan with me?"

Gabe grinned. "Naw, you wouldn't turn us down. Think of the health of my unborn son."

"Daughter," Joanna countered.

"This is perfect," Rose said with a new light in her eyes. "Ian, you can take over for Gabe. Now all we need is a lawyer to handle Joanna's—"

"Hannah has a law degree," Ian interjected. Only he said "law" much the way he might say "herpes."

Rubbing her hands together excitedly, Rose passed Ian the thick folder she had brought down from her office, as Gabe returned the lapel pin to Hannah.

"You can get started in the morning. Hannah," she continued as she turned so their eyes met. "Joanna can meet you at her office in the morning to go over whatever it is she does."

"Whoa!" Joanna called. "I can't just relinquish my practice to Hannah. She isn't even licensed to practice in this state."

Rose brushed that concern aside with her hand. "She doesn't have to try your cases, but she seems like a bright girl. I'm sure she can keep your clients happy while you rest. She can get a bunch of those continuance things or whatever you lawyers do to procrastinate until you come back. Don't argue, Joanna. This is what your doctor ordered and it seems to me that Hannah has arrived just in time—for you and your baby."

"No," Hannah said as she began placing her papers back in her folder. "I came here to find my mother. I wouldn't feel comfortable taking advantage of you all, especially since it appears I've been making some pretty terrible accusations. Thanks, but I'll think of another way."

"Quitting?" Ian asked, almost taunting in his tone. His blue-gray eyes shone with challenge.

"I don't quit. But I've obviously been given false information, so now I have to start all over again."

"Starting over sounds like just what Ian needs, as well," Gabe said in a stage whisper. It earned him a vicious glare.

Joanna looked at her with pleading eyes. "C'mon, Hannah, let Ian help you."

"Why should I?"

Ian's expression dawdled between arrogance and confidence. "Because I'm good."

Chapter Three

"She's here."

"Who is *she?* And I thought I told you not to call me here!"

After wiping his brow with a monogrammed handkerchief, he leaned his head back against the privacy shield of the public telephone on East Bay Street. "My man followed her from New Orleans. She's already found Rose Butler."

"Butler?" the man repeated.

"Yeah," he said as he looked around to make sure no one could hear him. "But her name is Porter now. Don't you remember that story last year about the woman who killed her ex-husband, then the cops found out it wasn't her? Rose Porter was the original woman they arrested."

"*That* Rose Butler."

"Porter," the man corrected into the receiver. "I know she'll remember me even though it's been more than thirty years. I'm in the alley next to the restaurant she owns. I can see her and some other people inside. Hannah Bailey is one of those people."

"Why are you telling me all this?" he asked, making no attempt to hide the contempt in his voice.

"If Miss Bailey found Rose, she'll find us!" he argued. "None of us can afford that."

"Then take care of it and don't call back unless it's to tell me that Hannah Bailey is no longer a problem for us. Do you understand?"

"Do *you* understand that means I might have to kill her?"

"I want her out of the picture. I don't really care how you do it, and I certainly don't want to know the details."

"What about the others?" he fairly pleaded. "I wasn't the only one involved."

"Do what you want. I'm out of it."

"That's what you think," he muttered as he slammed down the receiver and went back to his illegally parked, cream-colored Lincoln.

"I COULDN'T POSSIBLY do that," Hannah insisted. She was perched atop one of the two dozen bar stools that rimmed the horseshoe-shaped bar. Shelby Tanner was to her left, looking just a little pregnant and a lot nauseous. Her two small children, Chad and Cassidy, were giggling as they chased each other around the maze of empty tables.

"Of course you can," Shelby said as she slid a set of keys across the polished wood of the bar. "J.D. and Tory are in Miami, and their condo is just sitting there empty."

Hannah frowned with indecision. "But they

don't even know me." *You don't know me, either,* she added silently. "Surely they would object to a total stranger living in their house while they're away."

Rose came in then, followed by a woman Hannah judged to be somewhere between forty and fifty. A badge pinned to the white blouse of her waitress's uniform read Joleen, and she was looking at Hannah with startled brown eyes. Joleen seemed to be staring, but then again, Hannah was doing some staring of her own—at Rose. Joleen was the complete opposite of Rose Porter's flashy appearance.

"Did you give her the keys?" Rose directed her question to Shelby, who nodded her head. Even that small motion seemed to turn Shelby's pretty face a deeper shade of green.

Placing her hands where a wide black patent-leather belt cinched her small waist, Rose shot Hannah an impatient look. "Then why are you still here?" she groused.

Hannah didn't answer right away because she was cognizant that Joleen was still staring, probably waiting for an introduction. Joleen struck Hannah as the type who waited to be spoken to before she dared open her mouth. She didn't exactly exude self-confidence, but then, she was with Rose, who seemed to have more confidence in her little finger than most folks had in their entire body.

"I spoke to my son last night and he said you were welcome to use the condo," Rose said. "He and Tory will be in Miami for months. You'll just have to put up with their useless real-estate agent dragging folks in and out every so often." Rose turned slightly so that she faced Joleen. "At least say hello," she chided her employee. When Joleen offered nothing more than a half smile, Rose uttered a rather colorful word. "If you aren't going to be social, then start setup. And where is Susan?" Rose asked after she looked around and saw only Shelby's children in the restaurant.

Shelby took a sip of water, then said, "Her car's karma is off kilter." Her tone indicated she didn't find the explanation the least bit odd.

Hannah smiled when she recalled the very peculiar waitress Susan, as Joleen slipped soundlessly back through the double doors to the kitchen. Rose was certainly *acting* as if she couldn't possibly be Hannah's biological mother.

Rose rolled her eyes. "I didn't know cars had karmas."

"Don't worry," Shelby said. "Dylan is picking her up on his way here to get me and the kids. I have a doctor's appointment this morning."

Apparently, both Chad and Cassidy had heard their mother's plans and began a whining chorus of reasons why they didn't want to go sit in some doctor's office. Chad also added that if the new baby was another girl, he was going to buy his own house where there weren't so many girls.

"You'll grow out of that," Ian MacPhearson said as he entered through the kitchen. Lifting Chad and Cassidy, he tucked each child against his powerful body as if they were footballs and began spinning them.

They squealed with delight as Hannah looked on, mesmerized by Ian's ease with the small children. Somehow she had not expected him to be the type to spontaneously play with children. Her brain immediately conjured up images of Ian as a family man, all settled down with a quaint house with a fence and a dog. His weekends would be devoted to cutting the grass and trimming hedges, while his wife was busy inside cooking his favorite foods. What if...? her mind mused. Maybe he had children of his own. Maybe he was married. She quickly checked the ring finger of his left hand. It was bare, but that didn't mean anything. Some men didn't wear wedding bands.

But a man that looked as good as Ian should be wearing one if he was married. Heck, if he was married, he should have that fact tattooed on his forehead, she thought. Hannah blinked, trying to get her brain to stop thinking about how attractive he was. After a couple of seconds, she realized it was like trying to forget to breathe.

The warm smile he offered reached his eyes. "How are you, Miss Bailey?"

"Hannah," she corrected. The word had come out in some high pitch even she didn't recognize. "I'm fine, and you?"

Under the strong protests of Chad and Cassidy, Ian put the children down and walked in her direction. "The Omni has great accommodations," he answered. "Room service and a hot soak in a Jacuzzi is a wonderful way to start the day."

"Expensive, too," Rose interjected. "Staying

at a fancy place like that is a waste of good money, if you ask me."

Ian's grin suggested that he hadn't asked and didn't much care if Rose approved or not. "I enjoy staying at places like the Omni when I'm away from home."

He took the bar stool next to Hannah. The faint scent of soap mingled with the strong smell of coffee. Reaching around her, Ian took one of the mugs. His shoulder brushed hers for just a fraction of a second, but the sensation lasted longer than it took for him to pour himself coffee from the carafe.

Hugging her cup with unsteady hands, Hannah intentionally kept her eyes glued to the shelves of liquor bottles on the mirrored wall behind the bar. "No Jacuzzis in Montana?"

"I live a rather...simple life on the ranch." He took a sip of coffee without adding cream or sugar.

Funny, she thought, she never noticed details like that. Why was she suddenly so attuned to this man's every move, action or reaction?

"What about you?" he asked.

Hannah felt heat rush to her cheeks. "I have a house in the garden district in New Orleans."

Ian let out a slow whistle. "That's pretty pricey."

She turned away from Ian to watch the strangely mute Joleen enter, carrying a tray laden with salt and pepper mills. The waitress proceeded to arrange the items on each table, framing the still-empty bud vases. "It was my parents' house."

"What about before they passed away?"

Hannah turned and held his gaze. "I have always lived there."

Ian seemed to do his best to quell a smile. Joleen dropped a salt mill, to the delight of Chad, who began to do a little soft-shoe number in the spilled salt. Rose simply said, "What has gotten into you today, Joleen? Geez, you must have gotten up on the wrong side of the bed."

"Sorry," Joleen mumbled as she scurried off, probably to get something to clean up the salt before Chad—and now Cassidy—spread it from one end of the restaurant to the other. Silently, Hannah wished her luck. The Tanner children appeared rather wild. Her parents would never have allowed her to behave in such fashion.

As if reading her thoughts, Rose asked, "You must have gotten along well with your folks if you never left home."

Hannah smiled as her heart felt that tiny twang of pain that seemed to be lessening with time. "Very well. Which is the main reason I was so shocked to find out I was adopted, that my whole life with them had been a lie."

"Maybe they had a good reason for not telling you." Hannah and the others turned at the unexpected sound of Joleen's voice as she returned with broom and dustpan in hand.

"Like what?" Hannah asked.

Joleen shrugged. "I wouldn't know. But it seems to me that if they wanted you to come to

Charleston to look for your biological mother, they would have explained it all to you when they were still around.'' Joleen stood and left, using the excuse that she needed a damp cloth to finish the cleanup.

Shelby gave her children instructions to stay away from the few remaining crystals of salt. Instructions that were neither followed nor repeated. Apparently, the rumors were true. Shelby Tanner would never be named disciplinarian of the year. Of course, her children were so adorable and Shelby looked so ill that Hannah could fully understand why the woman was in no mood to argue the point with a toddler and a three-year-old.

In fact, she was amazed that Shelby had called her motel and summoned her to the Rose Tattoo earlier that morning. She had been expecting Joanna to call about the possibility of Hannah helping out, so Joanna could follow her doctor's orders to rest.

Since the unexpected summons from Shelby, Hannah spent the drive over from the less-expensive suburb of Mount Pleasant convinced that Rose had had a change of heart and was now willing to acknowledge Hannah's proof that Rose was her biological mother. Even the gas-guzzling tan car that had tailgated her hadn't deterred her growing anticipation. Under normal circumstances, Hannah would have slowed her car just to teach the tailgating jerk a lesson. But she had been far too excited to give some rude man a much-deserved lesson.

Using a crumpled map, Hannah had found the

Rose Tattoo more easily this time. On her first visit, she had not been prepared for the one-way streets or the mandatory turn lanes, and had gotten hopelessly lost. Charleston was nothing like New Orleans.

It wasn't long after her arrival that Shelby had revealed the real reason for the invitation.

Ignoring Ian for a minute, which was no easy task, Hannah studied Rose—her coloring, the way she walked, her hands, the habit she had of patting her teased coif. She saw nothing in Rose that indicated a biological link between them. Maybe Hannah favored her father. That would explain the birth certificate and the personal items her parents had secreted away for more than thirty years. The night before, the group had almost convinced her that her birth certificate and the other item were bogus. However, after a fitful night, she was no longer convinced that Rose should be dismissed so easily.

"Did they?"

Shaking her head as she returned to the present, Hannah met Ian's probing gaze and asked, "Did they what?"

"Did your parents ever do anything that might have led you to believe you were adopted? You know," he prompted, pausing to down the last of his coffee. "Have secret meetings when they registered you for school? Maybe asked you to leave the room when they spoke to your doctor?"

After a few minutes of thinking back over her thirty-one years, Hannah nodded. "I always thought they excluded me from things because they were overprotective in general."

"Let's get those invoices done so you can get home," Rose said to Shelby. "Hannah, take the keys and move into the condo. I'm not your mother, but I am a businesswoman. Paying rent to some motel, even a cheap one—" she stopped and sent a searing stare in Ian's direction "—can drain your bank account pretty darned quick. If you meant what you said about sticking around to find out who your mother is, save yourself a few bucks." Rose was now yelling over the sound of Joleen vacuuming.

"Would you be willing to take a blood test?" Hannah asked the second the notion popped into her mind. "DNA takes time, but it is very accurate."

Rose's shrug was almost bored, then she responded, "Sure."

Rose and Shelby excused themselves and went upstairs to their office. Joleen and her hand-held vacuum left a second later. Hannah and Ian remained, both staring at the set of keys Shelby had left on the bar.

Rose had agreed too easily to taking a test, Hannah mused. Either she was telling the truth and she wasn't Hannah's mother, or she was a smooth liar. Hannah tried to concentrate on her misgivings, but the squeals and hoots of the Tanner children, who had moved their game of tag onto the side porch, intruded on her thoughts.

Switching gears, Hannah turned her attention to the man beside her. Admitting to herself that it was hard to be next to this man was the easy part. Not letting him see just how he affected her was another matter altogether. He had this kind of magnetic appeal that Hannah had always read about but never truly believed. At least, not until his slightly callused hand brushed her fingers when they reached for the coffee carafe at the same time. She was in such a hurry to avoid his touch that she jerked her hand back and managed to spill the remainder of her coffee all down the front of her pale green blouse. She let out a muffled curse, which apparently amused Ian. His very masculine laughter did little to make her feel better.

"I'm never clumsy," she muttered as she dabbed at the coffee stain that would probably render the silk blouse unwearable.

Ian effortlessly vaulted the foot-and-a-half width of the bar and produced several napkins. When he made a move as if to blot the dampness where her blouse opened, revealing a modest implication of cleavage, Hannah snatched the towel away and said, "I have this rule about men I don't know touching me."

He gave her a grin that bordered on an amused leer. "I was only trying to help." His tone fell well short of sincerity.

Hannah blotted herself with the towel while she pretended the sexiness of his voice wasn't sending waves of heated awareness pulsing through her. *Get a grip!* she admonished silently. *He's just a man. Okay, so he's an incredibly attractive man, possibly the most gorgeous man you've ever seen, but remember why you're here.*

He came back around the bar, his boots scraping slightly with each stride. "I don't think you're clumsy," he said. "I'd say *skittish* was a better word. Do I make you nervous, Hannah?" His voice dropped to a deep, sexy drawl by the end of the question.

Collecting her composure, Hannah braved the task of meeting his gaze. Ian had light eyes that seemed to change from gray to blue upon silent command. Gray, she was learning, was definitely the come-on color. Everything about Ian appeared to be an open invitation—from the lazy half smile to the relaxed way he leaned against the bar, chewing on a plastic drink stirrer as if he intended to draw her attention to his mouth.

Hormones won out over intellect, and Hannah's eyes dropped lower. She knew then and there that Ian MacPhearson hadn't been born, he had been lovingly and perfectly sculpted. Each feature of his face was perfectly symmetrical. Even the sensual cleft in his chin was centered beneath lips that were neither full nor thin, just...perfect. His black eyebrows emphasized eyes that needed no such assistance. It was those eyes that called to her. His lashes were the same inky black as his thick hair and the faint stubble on his chin. She couldn't decide if the facial hair was a fashion thing or if he'd just forgone shaving that morning. If he had a physical fault or a flaw, she sure couldn't find it.

"You're staring," he said.

Hannah could feel her cheeks warm and knew from experience that they were probably red and blotchy. In her thirty-one years, she had yet to master the ability to keep blood from rushing to her face whenever she felt embarrassed or angry or both. It was one of the reasons she had opted to focus on legal research. In law school her classmates had dubbed her "the Blushing Barrister," and she'd never forgotten that.

"I'm supposed to meet with Joanna here this morning, and I was just wondering what you're doing here."

His smile told her he hadn't bought her little lie. "I'm supposed to be helping you find your biological mother so that my friend and his wife can get away for a while. Remember that conversation last night?"

Hannah simply nodded. Maybe she should tell him here and now that she was having second thoughts.

Ian's head tilted slightly as his eyes roamed over her face. "If I admit that I find you an incredibly beautiful woman, everything will be out in the open. Does that put you at ease?"

"No," she said on a little laugh as she lowered her head. "It actually makes me more uncomfortable."

"Men don't tell you you're beautiful?" he teased. "Or do you like to play coy and shy with men?"

Feeling a tad more relaxed, she met his eyes. "I don't play games with anyone, men included.

I also don't run around telling total strangers I think they're attractive."

He shrugged as if he had expected her answer. "I didn't know there was a time-line rule regarding when it is okay for a man to tell a woman she's attractive."

Hannah laughed. "I guess I did make it sound like there's some rule book we're supposed to be following. But, truth be told, it has been a while since a man has given me a compliment."

"That's hard to believe. I live out in the middle of nowhere, and even I've had a few women compliment me over the years." His chest puffed out just a fraction.

Hannah grinned up at him, battling a smile as she said, "Sex phone operators don't count."

Chapter Four

"That was a very low blow," Ian said, though the charming grin that accompanied the words made it perfectly clear that he had taken her remark for exactly what it was—a joke.

Before Ian could say another word, the Tanner children came screaming through the restaurant. Chad's, "Daddy!" was intelligible. Cassidy's eighteen-month-old vocabulary wasn't quite as clear, but she outran her older brother and raced full force into the legs of the tall, attractive man who had just unlocked the front door.

Hannah smiled, realizing instantly that she was looking at the adult version of Chad, which meant the new arrival was Dylan, Shelby's husband. He proceeded to hug, kiss and tickle each child until finally Chad and Cassidy decided they wanted to go back to their game on the side porch.

"Five minutes, guys!" he called, though he got no response. It was then that he turned his attention to Hannah, who was still seated on the bar stool, and Ian, who had risen and made a move toward the man. "I thought it might be you,"

Dylan said as he gave Ian a very familiar pat on the back as they shook hands.

The two men seemed to take a few seconds to size each other up, which indicated to Hannah that they probably knew each other but hadn't kept in touch.

"I only met your wife this morning," Ian told him. "I was thinking you might be her husband. How many Dylan Tanners can there be at ATF?"

Dylan gave Ian's shoulder one of those pretend punches and said, "They don't need but one, MacPhearson."

Hannah watched the men with a kind of fascination. She couldn't think of a friend with whom she had ever lost touch. Even the ones who had left Louisiana, she still called or wrote to regularly. Friends were important to her. She couldn't fathom letting any of them fade from her life.

Dylan playfully shoved Ian aside. As he came over to where Hannah was seated, she tried to tilt her body in such a way that he wouldn't notice the coffee stain on her shirt. Whether it was the polite way he shook her hand, or the gallant way he kept his distance as he introduced himself, Dylan Tanner's body language flashed happily married like a brilliant neon sign. Especially when he did a quick search of the room and failed to find his wife.

"Is she in the bathroom?" he asked, his angled face a mask of concern.

"She's upstairs," Hannah told him. "She's

easy to spot—the lovely woman with the rather pronounced green pallor.''

Dylan looked guilty. ''It wasn't like this with Cassidy,'' he said. ''The doctor swears it will pass, but I'm really worried about her.''

Ian moved over and placed a sympathetic hand on Dylan's shoulder. ''Shelby seems to be having a rough time of it. I'll bet she won't let you get within twenty feet of her for three or four years after this ordeal.''

Dylan gave Ian a baleful glare. ''At the risk of being indelicate in front of Miss Bailey, I can guarantee Shelby's...*interest* usually returns when she's still in the delivery room.'' Dylan's grin was purely lecherous. ''Or do I need to remind you that Chad and Cassidy are only eighteen months apart. This one will be here before Cassidy is two. So, my long-lost instructor—'' Dylan paused to sigh ''—don't waste any sleep over my love life.''

Ian laughed as he nodded. ''You've been a busy man these past...what's it been, six, seven years?''

''Seven,'' Dylan answered. ''Though sitting through that seminar you gave at the Pentagon felt like it was about a decade long.''

Ian scoffed. ''I'll bet you learned more in that week than you learned during your entire time at the academy.''

Dylan gave a shrug of silent surrender. ''Okay, so you were interesting and you did teach me a lot about investigative techniques. Especially undercover work.''

''Is that what you did for the CIA?'' Hannah asked. ''You were a teacher?''

''Teacher?'' Dylan repeated. ''Try hero.''

Dipping his head, Ian traced a knot in the wood flooring, clearly embarrassed. ''He's exaggerating,'' Ian said on a near whisper.

Hannah thought it rather cute that Ian was incapable of accepting praise. There was something intriguing about this new side of him. If it was possible, seeing this new vulnerable, humble side of him made him even more appealing, she thought as she watched him closely.

''I am not exaggerating,'' Dylan insisted. ''This man and his partner were the *best* at infiltrating drug rings and stopping the shipments before they could reach this country.''

Hannah was impressed. Ian just hung his head and pretended great interest in the grain pattern of the floor planks. ''I think that makes you a hero,'' she said with genuine admiration. ''I'd also bet that doing that sort of work would be draining. Never knowing when your cover would be blown. I think you're being humble for no reason—you should be proud of yourself. Keeping drugs from ever reaching our streets is quite an accomplishment, Ian. You should be proud.''

''She's right, you know,'' Dylan added. ''You were one hell of a good agent.'' Dylan's expression grew a bit playful. ''Since you are no longer subject to the restrictions of an agency code of ethics, would you mind going out to the alley and getting that fat joker to move his car? I couldn't get to the lot and neither will the lunch patrons if he doesn't move."

"Sorry, Dylan, no can do. These days I leave the enforcement of laws up to guys like you."

"Then will you at least come upstairs with me and protect me when I explain to Shelby that Susan refused to come inside because she's sensing some sort of warning from the other side?"

All three laughed.

"I thought it was her car that was having karma troubles," Hannah offered.

"It was," Dylan admitted. "Only now she thinks the car breaking down was a sign from the other world for her to stay at home."

"She really is a few sandwiches shy of a picnic, isn't she?" Ian asked.

Dylan just shrugged. "She's definitely weird, but she is one of the kindest people I have ever known." Dylan stroked his chin. "As a matter of fact, Susan reminds me a little bit of your partner, what was her name? The one who was so nice, not to mention easy on the eyes."

Hannah could only describe Ian's reaction as like watching a vault slam, then seal shut. "Her name was Carmen and she died five years ago." Ian pivoted and went toward the front door. "Maybe I will go out into the alley and explain the concept of a no-parking zone to your friend, after all."

He slammed the door with enough force to rattle the stained-glass oval inlay. Hannah and Dylan looked at each other, apparently both totally unprepared for Ian's sudden change in mood.

"What was that all about?" Hannah asked as she watched Ian's profile disappear through the beveled glass picture window at the front of the restaurant.

"Beats me," Dylan answered. After checking his watch, he went behind the bar and dialed the telephone. She could tell he was speaking to his wife.

His facial expression as well as his tone communicated more than just his desire for Shelby to come down to leave for the doctor's office. It conveyed a love so strong and pure that it very nearly brought tears to Hannah's eyes. It was ludicrous and she silently chided herself for suddenly turning into a bundle of emotions. She blamed it on lack of sleep.

Just as Shelby herded her children through the dining room, Gabe, Joanna and a frightful Susan came through the double kitchen doors. A bit surprisingly, Ian wasn't among them. If they came through the kitchen, they must have used the alley entrance, which meant Ian had convinced the illegally parked driver to move. *So where is he?*

Getting Chad and Cassidy under control and out to the car took several minutes. Each child was given a quarter and permitted to select one Elvis Presley tune from the jukebox. Under the terms of the plea bargain, they would then leave quietly and cooperatively.

Chad picked "Jailhouse Rock" and amused Hannah as he lip-synched along with the song. The blue-eyed, black-haired little boy even had a few of Elvis's famous hip shakes down pat.

"Rose taught him that," Shelby whispered. "Thanks to my business partner, my son now says he wants to be an Elvis impersonator when he grows up."

Hannah chuckled. "Look on the bright side, you won't have to put away money for college."

Shelby's smile was weak but heartfelt. Hannah was amazed by how at ease she felt with these people. Even though she wasn't completely convinced of Rose's veracity, she couldn't help but like the woman and all the people associated with her.

Cassidy's selection was "Return to Sender," and she did her best to imitate Elvis as her brother had done. Everyone applauded when the performance was finished. Everyone except Cassidy Tanner. As soon as Dylan went to pick her up, she ran from him, giggling even as her father threatened punishment until he finally was able to nab the squirming little girl. The sounds of Cassidy screaming could still be heard a short while after the Tanner family had left the building.

Gabe let out a long breath, turned to Joanna and said, "Tell me again why we wanted to have a baby?"

Joanna's response was a playful swat to her husband's arm. "We'll be strong, Gabe. I know we can handle it. After all, it will be two against one."

"Poor Dylan," Gabe lamented. "In a few months he'll be outnumbered and none of us will be safe."

"Stop it, you two," Rose admonished, though

a twinkle of amusement danced in her eyes. ''Just you wait until you're the parents, and we'll see how holier than thou you are then.'' Rose next turned her attention to Susan, who had moved to the doors leading to the side porch and was craning her neck to peer outside.

Hannah wondered if Ian was still out there with the driver of the illegally parked car, so she moved quickly to where Susan was standing.

''He's gone,'' Susan said in a near whisper. ''But I'm sensing a great deal of hostility and danger in the space he occupied.''

''Are you talking about Ian?'' Hannah asked.

Without abandoning her search for the unknown, Susan just shook her head. ''Not Ian, but I did see him drive off. *Him.*''

''Unless by 'Him' you meant the good Lord has returned to earth,'' Rose called, ''would you mind getting to work. Lunch is only ninety minutes from now.''

Hannah moved away from the porch doors just as Rose pushed her way into the kitchen. One of the doors remained open, so Hannah was able to see into the kitchen.

''Has anyone seen Mickey?'' she yelled.

Hannah heard a few of the busboys mumble in the negative and an elderly man who was icing a cake to perfection shook his head. The question was repeated a minute or so later when Joleen and a young waiter called Mark appeared in the kitchen.

''This is wonderful,'' Rose groused as she came around the bar and grabbed the telephone.

As she dialed, she looked up and saw Susan still standing guard against *Him.* "Go help with the salad setup, or you're fired," she said. This time her tone convinced Hannah—and apparently Susan—that she was serious. Still wearing a haunted look on her face, Susan went into the kitchen, closing the door behind her.

"Mickey!" Rose bellowed into the phone, "you should have been here by now."

Whatever was being said on the other end of the line did not please Rose, her angry expression made that crystal clear. She listened for less than a minute before she let loose with a string of rather colorful and disparaging descriptions of Mickey's abilities as a chef. The call ended with Rose promising him she would do everything in her power to see that Mickey didn't get work in the whole of Charleston so long as she had a breath left in her body.

When she slammed the receiver back on its cradle, she blew out a breath of frustration and shook her head. The action made her zebra earrings look as if they were cantering. "I can't believe that weasel quit without notice. Now what am I supposed to do?" Rose asked.

Gabe shrugged, but Joanna went racing from the room. Hannah assumed she was suffering the same fate as Shelby, so, being the only one willing to respond, she suggested Rose close the restaurant for the day.

From Rose's expression, Hannah got the feeling her idea wasn't an option. "I'd offer to help, but my best dish is peanut butter and jelly."

Rose looked at Gabe, who simply said, "I had a cook growing up and Joanna's no better. Why do you think we come here for dinner so often?"

"I was hoping it was to see me," Rose grumbled.

"I found it!" Joanna squealed as she half ran, half waddled back into the room. She was straightening and folding a page from the newspaper.

"I can't hire a chef out of the want ads," Rose said. "At least not one without references I can verify in the next thirty minutes."

"Look!" Joanna insisted as she tapped her finger on a portion of the page. Hannah moved to read over the smaller woman's shoulder. "This DeLancey Jones woman won the Medal of Honor from the Charleston Culinary Institute yesterday. The CCI doesn't give those out for nothing, and I'll bet we can find her and have her here in time for lunch."

Rose brightened immediately. "I'm going up to my office. Considering I've hired two of their graduates as interns, I'll bet they'll give me her phone number."

Gabe gave his wife a short but meaningful kiss on the forehead. "That was fast thinking, Mrs. Langston."

"Ms. Boudreaux," she corrected. "Until the baby comes, I get to keep my identity, that was the deal."

"That was *your* deal," he teased. "If I—"

Gabe was interrupted by a distinct chirping sound that seemed to be coming from Joanna's purse. Joanna pulled a thin electronic organizer out of her bag and began reading.

"Who was Carmen?" Hannah asked Gabe.

The man's face froze, then his brows drew together questioningly. "Did Ian mention her?"

"Yes. Dylan inquired after her and the next minute Ian stormed out of here. I was just wondering," Hannah said, forcing her voice to sound conversational. "Dylan said she was Ian's partner?"

Gabe nodded. "She was, but that story is Ian's to tell, not mine."

Joanna saved Gabe from any further interrogation by Hannah when she reminded him that he had to take her and Hannah to her office now if they were going to have enough time to pack before they left.

"Yes, dear," Gabe said with a wink. To Hannah he said, "She only got pregnant because her organizer had it listed as an approved activity."

"Give it a rest, Langston," Joanna warned. "I'll bet Hannah has an organizer, too. Am I right?"

Feeling her cheeks flame, Hannah nodded, pulling a newer, fancier model from her purse and displaying it as Gabe exaggerated a groan.

"I'll follow you," Hannah suggested. "I've got to learn my way around the city."

"Ian will be helping you," Joanna said.

"He won't be helping me drive. Shouldn't we wait to see if Rose is able to get that Jones woman?"

Gabe and Joanna exchanged a look that was a

lot like a secret handshake. "I'm surprised DeLancey Jones isn't here already. My mother can be very persuasive," Gabe said.

"So persuasive that you won't even consider the possibility that she could be my mother?"

Gabe's smile was kind and surprisingly gentle for a man his size. "Believe me, if you were Rose's daughter, she'd be up on the roof shouting the fact to the whole town. Ian will find out how her name ended up on your birth certificate. He's really good, Hannah."

"I guess that's why he left without so much as saying goodbye," Hannah muttered.

"He's probably out trying to do that right now."

"Do what?" Hannah asked Gabe.

"Say goodbye."

Before Gabe could elaborate, Rose came back, skipping like a happy, carefree child. "Ms. DeLancey Jones will be here in time for the lunch crowd. I've got to go and call my suppliers and have some things delivered ASAP. And we're scrapping the menu and putting up chalkboards. DeLancey will fill in a list of offerings until she familiarizes herself with our regular menu. I sent Joleen out to buy the chalkboards." Rose paused from her elated monologue and frowned. "Joleen has been as quiet as a mouse lately. I think she's disgusted by Susan and her dead people's clothes, and now Susan is in the kitchen chattering non-stop about seeing a man in the alley with a bright red aura. I'd better speak to them. I can't afford to lose either one of them. Mark is a good waiter, but he isn't as good or as experienced as Joleen or Susan."

Joanna's organizer beeped again and Hannah decided she was glad. For some reason, she wasn't interested in the hirings and firings of the Rose Tattoo.

Had Carmen been more than just Ian's partner? As she walked to her car a step or two behind Gabe and his wife, she was troubled by two things. *I want to know who Ian is saying goodbye to. And I want to know how one man can make me lose focus in twenty-four short hours.*

Hannah followed Gabe's Mercedes as they took a series of side streets until they reached the Cooper River Bridge. It was at about that point that Hannah realized that a dark blue, four-door sedan was driving practically up her fender. She suddenly slammed on her brakes, forcing the blue car to do the same. Afraid she might lose her escorts, she sped up.

Once over the bridge, cityscape gave way to suburbs. Again Hannah followed as Gabe made a series of turns through what appeared to be a neighborhood. The blue four-door came right along with them. Recalling various news reports on the relatively new phenomenon called road rage, she suddenly regretted her actions on the bridge. Maybe the blue car was following her, its driver angry and ready to tell her just what he thought of her stepping on her brakes in heavy traffic in the middle of the span high above the Cooper River. Hopefully, he just wanted to scream at her. Hannah didn't want to think about the horror stories of people being shot for some real or imagined traffic infraction.

Gabe pulled the Mercedes into the driveway of a house in the shadows of the bridge. Much to Hannah's relief, the blue car kept going. Her five minutes of abject fear had been for naught; yet when she stepped from her rented compact, she felt her legs buckle just for a second.

Luckily, Gabe and Joanna were in the middle of a rather loud discussion on how long she planned to stay off work after the baby arrived. She was grateful that neither of them noticed that Hannah was a tad shaky.

After stepping through a door with Joanna Boudreaux, Attorney At Law painted on the glass, Hannah found herself in a small reception area. She couldn't picture Joanna as the type to cut lilacs and place them in a vase on the neat desk. She was right, because a woman with a cheerful, carefree manner stepped out from the door marked Private.

"I'm Tammy," she said as she came over to offer her hand. "I only work mornings, because I have three kids and an ex-husband who pays support about as regularly as we have earthquakes in South Carolina. I miss time every now and then because I sign up to go on field trips with my kids. If one of them is sick, I stay home." Her smile grew wider. "And Joanna never docks my pay."

Hannah had to laugh at the woman's straightforwardness. "I see. Well, I'm Hannah and I think it's great that Joanna is so generous and contemporary in her office policies."

Tammy laughed. "Don't give Joanna too much credit, I type out my paycheck, she just signs it." Tammy spun around and took a deep breath of the freshly cut flowers, then said, "I've given myself two raises this year. No telling what I'll do while she's off playing on some exotic beach."

"I'm not playing, I'm *enduring*. Obviously you've forgotten what it's like to be pregnant," Joanna huffed. "Please excuse Tammy. She's as smart as her mouth or I would have fired her years ago."

"Would not," Tammy said as she reached for a small stack of pink message slips. "I put the urgent one on top and the rest can wait till you get Hannah up to speed."

"C'mon, Tammy. Let's go out for a doughnut while my darling wife and Hannah talk."

Tammy eyed her boss's husband. "Who's paying?"

"Me."

"Deal," Tammy said. Lifting the receiver, she punched a bunch of numbers on the keypad, then turned to Joanna and said, "We're on voice mail, so don't bother if the phone rings. I put the stuff the dry cleaner delivered by your suitcases, so all you have left to do is add the personal stuff."

"Thanks, Tammy," Joanna said, genuine fondness in her tone.

While Joanna dealt with her one urgent matter, Hannah was instantly drawn to the framed picture that hung above a group of filing cabinets. Carpeting silenced her footsteps as she moved over for a closer look. It was the same picture from the newspaper clipping she had found among her mother's things, only this was the original glossy photo. Joanna must have gotten it directly from the photographer. Now that she had met Rose, she concentrated on the others in the photograph. Joleen, Susan, Mark, and the now-former chef Mickey were standing behind Rose. Joanna, Gabe, Dylan, Shelby and Kendall Revel, a woman who bore a slight resemblance to Rose, were to the right. To the left stood J.D., Wesley, Destiny Talbott and an attractive man she had not yet met but recalled his name as being Jonas Revel from the caption under her copy of the clipping. No matter how long she looked, Rose was obviously the center of the photograph. Her face was focused better than the others. "This picture is about Rose."

"Of course it is," Joanna said.

Hannah turned, not realizing she had vocalized her thought. "Sorry. I'm still trying to understand why this picture was important to my mother."

"Maybe she knew Joe Don," Joanna suggested as she took her seat and began to write on a legal pad. "You mentioned that your parents used to bring you here on vacation—perhaps they visited the Rose Tattoo back then. I think it was called the Rusty Nail before Rose bought it."

Hannah nodded at the possibility. "Do you know everyone in the picture?"

"Mmm-hmm," Joanna mumbled as she continued to make notes. "If you're thinking one of them could be your father, you're way off base. None of them are old enough."

"What about Mark, or Jonas or Mickey? Maybe I share a biological father with one of them."

Joanna looked up from her task and smiled. "There is no way you could share DNA with Mickey since his family tree doesn't fork. I've met Mark's parents and they're nice people. Maybe you and Ian can check them out. I've got a file on everyone who worked at the Rose Tattoo when Joe Don was murdered. I didn't go so far as to check parents of employees, because I thought it was a waste of Gabe and J.D.'s money. If Rose is willing to waive privilege, get it in writing. Then feel free to look your fill."

"Thank you," Hannah said. She was touched to think Joanna was this willing to help her out. "Gabe and J.D. paid for Rose's defense? Her sons certainly are devoted to her."

Hannah was forced to wait until Joanna finished her list until the other woman explained. "At the time, we all thought Gabe was just a private detective killing time, no pun intended."

"You mean Rose didn't even know her own child?"

"It had been thirty some years, Hannah. Like you, Gabe was raised in a loving family, until his parents died and he opted to sell Langston Publishing, which didn't sit too well with the fringe relations."

"Whoa," Hannah said, raising her hands. "He's one of *those* Langstons?"

"Yep."

"Then, if you don't mind me asking, why are you juggling work and the impending birth of your baby?"

Joanna frowned. "I was sorta hoping you'd be on my side."

"I didn't know I was taking a side."

"Gabe and I can't seem to agree as to what age this baby has to be before I return to work full-time." Joanna's smile was rather whimsical. "It reminds me of when we first met."

"You were pregnant when—"

"No, it wasn't like that. Gabe was rammed down my throat by Rose and Shelby. If I wanted the case, Gabe came along as sort of a package deal. We disagreed on just about everything from the very start. Unless you count the immediate chemistry. My heart actually fluttered the first time I saw him. I tried to ignore the chemistry, since we didn't seem to get along. Then we had this period of calm when I fell for him—and I mean hard. Then he springs the truth on me."

"Which truth?"

"That he was Rose's son."

Hannah was stunned. "You mean you worked together day in and day out and he never confided in you?"

"Exactly right. And he only told me to keep me from walking off the case in the middle of the trial."

"So how did you end up married to him?" Hannah asked, thinking of the hurt and betrayal she had suffered when she had learned of her parents' long-held secret.

"I knew I loved him more than anything."

"It was that simple?" Hannah asked. "Love conquered all?"

Joanna was pensive for a minute before saying, "Only when it's the right love from the right man." Joanna's expression changed abruptly. Her face was slightly swollen due to her condition, and her mischievous grin made her look like a sorority sister planning an event for rush week. "Got anybody back in New Orleans?"

"My dog, Spence, is in a kennel," Hannah admitted. "Nothing on two legs is waiting for my return, if that's what you're asking."

"Then watch out for Rose. She can be dangerous in situations like this."

"What situation?"

"You and Ian."

Hannah swallowed hard. "Me and Ian what? Together? He lives like a hermit in some remote part of a state that I don't think ever gets temperatures above freezing. He's charming, gorgeous, has a great sense of humor, a body to die for and seems intelligent, but any female with a breath left would notice those things about Ian. Even with all those wonderful qualities, I still have nothing in common with the man."

Joanna grinned and said, "Do you realize you just gave the textbook definition of chemistry between a man and a woman?"

Hannah felt herself blush from the roots of her hair to her toes. She wouldn't look the other woman in the eye as she spoke. "Even if that did sound like I feel a chemistry with Ian—which I am not admitting—why would Rose care?"

"You don't know Rose."

Chapter Five

The underside of his car scraped as he drove too quickly into the narrow alleyway between the Rose Tattoo and the Charleston single house next door, which was still a private residence. Ian parked in the small lot adjacent to the dependency, which, Rose had informed him, had been the summer kitchen and servants' quarters when the house was built around the time of the Civil War. Rose and Shelby had since turned it into a small club where local and nationally recognized talent entertained on weekends.

His footsteps echoed in the cavernous space between the buildings as he walked toward the rear entrance.

Going through a heavy door marked Employees Only, he was greeted by the barrage of mouth-watering smells from the kitchen. Ian was forced to turn sideways in order to pass by stacks of boxes and crates of fresh fruits and vegetables—apparently recent deliveries—in order to get to the flight of stairs that led to the second story.

As he walked toward Rose's office, he noted

the second floor was home to a bathroom, a storage room and the large office that Rose and Shelby shared. He suspected the offices had once been two or three smaller rooms, converted to accommodate desks, credenzas, file cabinets and an assortment of baby paraphernalia.

Rose's side of the room could only be described as organized clutter. He didn't need to be told which desk belonged to the flamboyant woman. The painting of Elvis Presley on black velvet that hung behind one of the desks was a dead giveaway. Then there were the framed photographs of Rose visiting Graceland and a host of Elvis memorabilia scattered around.

Shelby Tanner's side of the room was a completely different matter. It was all soft pastels and framed pictures of her husband and children. They weren't those phony-looking, staged portraits, either. They were natural, spontaneous moments captured forever. Simply by looking at them, it was instantly apparent that the Tanners were a very happy couple. For a split second, Ian envisioned one of those frames holding a picture of his son or daughter. The child he had never had an opportunity to know.

After offering a warm greeting, Shelby walked across a thick area rug to take a seat behind her large nineteenth-century desk. Giant beveled glass windows were behind her desk, trimmed in fabric the same shade of blue as her eyes. A mahogany credenza dominated the other wall.

"We got through lunch without a hitch,"

Shelby told him. "Let's hope our new chef works the same magic at dinner."

Seeing the fatigue around her eyes, Ian asked, "Can't Rose handle dinner? You look tired."

Shelby's smile was as soft as her lilting Southern drawl. "I've just got a few purchase orders to take care of, then I'm going home."

"Good." Ian said. Turning to clear a place to lean against the credenza, he moved a collage of framed photographs of Shelby's children and Rose's adult sons and their wives. It appeared by the condition of the frames that there were three recent additions to the montage. One was silver and engraved with the names Jonas and Kendall; it included a recent wedding date. Rose's niece. The next was also a wedding picture, taken at a ceremony downstairs in front of the massive stone fireplace. He had seen the picture before; in fact, he had a copy of it. Joanna had been a beautiful bride with all that wild red hair and skin as pale and flawless as the traditional dress she had worn for the special occasion. The third picture was an eight-by-ten of a newborn with its parents. He thought the bald baby looked like Fred Mertz from the "I Love Lucy" show, but so did most babies, in his opinion. An opinion he kept to himself, given present company.

If he had to use a single word to describe Shelby's side of the room, it would be feminine. The word *kitsch* came to mind when he surveyed the things Rose had chosen to surround herself with during her long hours at work. But it was the coffee mug in the shape of Elvis Presley's head that cinched it for him.

"Hello?"

Ian stopped his impromptu survey and offered Shelby an apologetic smile. "Sorry, I was just doing a little comparison."

Her smile indicated that she had guessed his conclusions.

"How did someone like you hook up with someone like Rose?"

After putting down her pen, Shelby folded her hands neatly and looked him directly in the eyes. "At the time, I was pregnant with Chad, unmarried and I knew if I didn't invest the money I had made from selling my interests in my previous business, I'd never be able to raise Chad in a decent home."

Ian felt his eyebrows draw together. "Where was Dylan?"

"He was unaware of my condition. It wasn't until Chad was kidnapped that Dylan came back into my life."

He noticed some residual fear in her eyes when she said the word *kidnapped.* However, the fear was quickly replaced with an almost giddy happiness at the mere mention of her husband's name.

"I'm glad things worked out for you two," he said. Lifting one of the pictures that someone had matted and framed, he silently read the headlines and accompanying story of Rose's acquittal on the charge of murdering her ex-husband, Joe Don Porter. The article outlined the details of the murder and the trial, complete with a photograph. It was the same photograph Hannah had brought with her to Charleston.

Only this one was in glossy, full color, just like Rose, who was the focus of the picture. She was standing at the foot of the stairs in front of the Rose Tattoo. He knew that because, though the name of the restaurant was obscured by a tall man in chef's whites, the large picture window was clearly recognizable.

"Can you think of any reason why a woman in New Orleans would have a copy of this article?" he asked, not ready to share his new discovery with anyone but Rose and Hannah first. Not wanting to risk his facial expression giving away what was in his shirt pocket, he continued to study the details of the photograph.

"Dylan and I were talking last night, and we thought it might have something to do with Joe Don. That article is kind, to say the least. Joe Don was the type of man who always had several women...*friends*."

Ian almost laughed at the propriety of her description of the deceased. Shelby Tanner was a lady. So was Hannah. He felt his thoughts take a distinct turn just thinking about the blond beauty. While he wasn't exactly thrilled at being coerced into staying in Charleston to help the woman, he had to admit being in Hannah's company wasn't exactly painful. He also had to admit that for the first time in five years he was thinking thoughts he believed had died along with Carmen.

He cleared his thoughts by counting the

black-and-white marble tiles arranged in a checkerboard pattern in the photo. He'd been told this was one of the hallmarks of a Charleston single house. Gabe was easy for him to pick out among the dozen or so people gathered in the picture. What surprised him was how very much his friend looked like his half brother, J.D. He assumed the very pregnant woman next to J.D. was his wife, Tory, since J.D. had one hand pressed protectively against her swollen belly. He laughed to himself as he recalled Hannah's remark about there being something in the water at the Rose Tattoo. It appeared only Rose, Wesley's famous wife, Destiny Talbott, and the waitresses weren't in some stage of pregnancy. He didn't know how far along Shelby was, so she could have been included in the drank-the-water group, too.

There was a distinct resemblance between Gabe and Wesley Porter as well, though not as striking as the one between the two oldest sons. "Hannah doesn't look much like Rose's other children," Ian remarked. "They don't look like Rose either, so am I correct in assuming J.D. and Wesley both have their father's coloring?"

Shelby nodded. "I guess that shoots the Joe Don theory out the window. Hannah sure doesn't look anything like Joe Don's sons and—" Shelby lowered her voice "—I happen to know Rose's natural hair color is brown, but please don't repeat that. Rose guards her age and her hair color fiercely."

"I swear, your secret is safe," Ian teased as he made a cross over his heart. Once again he turned to the picture for some insight. Instead of her waitress's uniform, Susan Taylor was dressed in street clothes. He smiled because the ill-fitting, floral-print gauze skirt, striped shirt and scuffed boots made her look as if she had rolled a homeless person to get the clothes. He noted that her hair was quite different then, as well. It wasn't copper, it was a brilliant shade of purple, like grape Kool-Aid, and her nose wasn't pierced, or she wasn't wearing an earring—at least not in her nose. She must have had five or six earrings in each ear. It made him shiver just thinking about sticking things through the tender cartilage of his ear. As odd as it sounded, her new fashion choices, though morose, were an improvement over how she had looked a few months earlier.

There was also a stranger, who wasn't really focused in the photograph. The tall, leggy woman had her red hair pulled off her face. She was certainly pretty, but she had that aggressive, self-assured smugness that some men found attractive. Ian preferred just a hint of vulnerability—like Hannah possessed.

"Who is this?" Ian asked, holding out the photo and pointing to the woman. "She isn't in the copy of the picture that made it into the paper."

"That's Barbara Prather. She was pretty ticked off when they cropped her out of the shot. She's a friend of Susan's and just happened to be at the restaurant on the day they came to shoot the picture. Barbara wasn't involved in any part of the case, so they cut her out. She was hoping for some exposure since she owns her own ad agency. She's one of those any-publicity-is-good-publicity types."

He gave the Prather woman another once-over, mainly to compare her to Hannah. A couple of times he had seen Hannah display that controlled, calm expression. However, under that cool, determined visage, he was pretty sure there was also a healthy dose of wariness, which she was trying her best to camouflage. Since, by her own admission, Hannah had never lived on her own, he suspected that the sudden death of her parents had been a devastating event. He also guessed that this quest to find her biological mother was more of a coping mechanism than a true search for biological identity.

"You have to come and help!" a very frazzled Susan cried as she reached the office door.

"What's wrong?" Shelby asked as she hurriedly rose and came around her desk.

"It's Hannah," she began, but Ian didn't stick around to hear any more.

He bolted down the steps, taking them two or three at a time. He found Rose with her arms around Hannah, and he could tell by the way her slender shoulders were shaking that Hannah was crying.

Rose looked up and met his eyes, silently beckoning him. "Everything is okay now," Rose soothed as she gently held Hannah at arm's length. "Ian will go out and check the parking lot."

When he saw the tracks of the tears that had

spilled down from her wide, frightened eyes, his first instinct was to pull her into his embrace. But he knew that was just an emotional reaction, and emotional reactions could be deadly, so he asked, "What am I looking for?"

"A man in a green sports car," Hannah managed to say between gulps for air. "He followed me from my motel. He tried to run me off the road."

"It was *Him,*" Susan said with absolute conviction when she reached the bottom of the stairs. "I tried to warn you this morning, but—"

"Go play with your crystals or call the psychic hot line," Rose cut in, clearly annoyed with Susan's otherworldly suggestion. Turning to Ian, she asked, "Go take a look around, Ian, would you?"

Since Hannah didn't impress him as the kind of person given to hysterics, he exited the building. The first thing he noticed was the strong, pleasant scent of flowers from the garden next door. The second thing he noticed wasn't pleasant. Hannah's compact rental had a long dent and a gash filled with green paint near the front panel.

His whole body seemed to go into alert mode. Every sound, every scent, every motion, became a part of his consciousness. He made a thorough search of the grounds, both front and back, and even checked the dependency. He found nothing, saw no one.

Going back to Hannah's car and kneeling, he improvised by using a photograph he had brought along with him to scrape some of the green paint onto the backside of the picture. Maybe a lab analysis could discover the make and model of the car. Find the car and he might be able to find the driver. Of course, the odds of it being that simple were about a zillion to one, but stranger things had happened.

Careful not to crush the chips of paint, he went back into the restaurant and had one of the busboys wrap the chips in plastic. He then put the evidence in the same pocket as the photograph and asked the busboy where Hannah and Rose had gone.

Taking his time, he climbed the stairs and found Rose and Hannah in the office. Rose was pacing, Hannah was sipping what looked like brandy.

"Well?" Rose asked.

Hannah looked up at him with expectation in her big blue eyes. Ian shook his head. "I did take some paint samples from where the guy hit your car." Ian reluctantly took his eyes off Hannah's upturned face and looked to Rose. "Know anyone on the local police force who might do you a favor?"

Rose mentioned a Detective Ross, then said, "I'll tell him to meet you at J.D.'s condo. He'll do whatever you need done."

"Condo?" Ian repeated. "Did I miss something? I thought you were against the condo idea."

Rose gave Hannah a stern look and said, "Tell him."

Hannah seemed uncertain and hesitant. "It might just be my imagination."

"Tell him," Rose insisted.

Taking a fortifying breath, Hannah began wringing her hands and she kept her eyes lowered. "I think someone has been following me ever since I arrived in Charleston. So Rose thinks I'll be safer at J.D. and Tory's condo because there is security at the building."

Ian tugged at the fabric of his jeans so that he could crouch in front of Hannah, forcing her to meet his eyes. "You think?" he parroted.

"I'm not sure because I've never seen the driver, and it's always a different car."

"Usually," he began patiently, "if you're being tailed, it's the same car. *If* someone is following you, I wouldn't think he'd have the time or the opportunity to buy a new car for each outing."

A flash of annoyance sparked in her eyes. "I *know* that, which is why I haven't said anything to anyone until now."

"Tell me everything that happened up to the time the green car tried to run you off the road," Ian instructed.

Hannah took a swallow of her drink before beginning. "My motel was out of stamps, so I got directions to the closest post office."

"You were going out to buy stamps?" Ian asked, not certain he had heard her correctly.

She nodded. "For the postcards I wanted to send to my friends back home."

"You mean to tell me that in the middle of your search for your biological mother, you're sending postcards to your friends?"

Hannah glared at Ian. "You make it sound like

I was attempting to send a mail bomb. *Of course* I was sending postcards. My friends and I always send postcards when we're away from home."

Ian let out a long breath. "Your pen-pal mentality almost got you killed."

Hannah's glare turned into an expression of pure fury. She almost knocked him backward when she abruptly stood. "You might choose not to have friends, Mr. MacPhearson, but I don't live like a hermit. Your insinuation that this was somehow my fault is too stupid for words." She grabbed her purse off Rose's desk. "You can forget your plan, Rose. This man couldn't find his...*ears* with both hands."

Before she could make her escape, Ian grasped her arm. He was surprised by her smallness and stunned by his body's immediate reaction to touching her. "Hang on," he said. Sensing no change in her determination to leave, he added, "I might not be able to find my ears with both hands, but I have found something in reference to your birth certificate."

Hannah turned, tilting her head back to gaze up at him with anticipation. *Lord but this woman was mercurial!*

"Tell me!"

"What did you find?" Rose added.

Instead of releasing Hannah, he lifted his other hand and gently caressed the fabric covering her shoulders to her elbows. It was amazing to see the effect of his touch register in her eyes. They seemed to darken, and her lips parted as if she planned to say something. Instead, her tongue flicked out and moistened her lower lip. Ian found himself swallowing a groan and releasing her as if she had suddenly caught fire.

"I, um, went to the newspaper morgue this afternoon on a hunch," he said as he shifted positions in the hopes that his sudden and unexpected reaction to Hannah wouldn't be noticeable to the two women. It felt to him as if his heart was pounding against his ribs. Surely they could hear it, even at the distance of a couple of feet.

"What hunch?" Hannah asked. "Stop drawing this out, please?"

Ian reached into his shirt pocket and retrieved the photograph he had taken from the morgue. He didn't make a habit of stealing things, but he was fairly certain the newspaper wouldn't miss the picture, and he could always mail it back to them anonymously in a few months.

Hannah was holding the picture with Rose looking on. Hannah's expression was blank, but Rose smiled as she patted her hair. "This was taken when the place was called the Rusty Nail. I sure was thin back then." She sighed. "My waist would have made Scarlett O'Hara envious."

Hannah lifted her chin and met his eyes. "You found an old picture of Rose waiting tables back before she owned this place. I don't get the connection between this old picture and my birth certificate."

Ian came over and pointed to a banner strung across the mantel of the massive fireplace. "When were you born?" he asked.

"January 1, 1967."

"Thank you, Ian," Rose said. Then she gave Hannah a hug and said, "But I'd be happy to keep you around and pretend you're my daughter."

Hannah shrugged free of them both and said, "But I still don't get it. How does this picture prove Rose isn't my mother?"

"Look at the banner, Hannah," Ian said.

"Happy New Year," she read. "So what? It doesn't say what year."

He felt a pang of guilt being the one to vanquish her last hope, but it couldn't be helped. "Read the information on the back of the picture," he said. "This picture was used for a story on New Year's celebrations in Charleston."

"December 31, 1966," she said, her voice a mere whisper by the time she finished reading.

He watched as Hannah flipped the pictures over and took a long look at Rose's image. It would have been physically impossible for Rose to have been nine months' pregnant when the picture was taken. Impossible for her to have given birth to Hannah the next day.

Hannah clearly recognized that and said, "I'm sorry to have troubled you." She kept her eyes lowered, but there was a definite catch in her voice. "I apologize for any inconvenience to you or your family." Hannah slipped the picture onto Rose's desk. "Thank you, Ian. At least I know for certain that coming here was a wild-goose chase."

"How can you say that?" Ian asked.

She looked at him through the veil of her lashes. "I think I only wanted to find my biological mother so I could blame someone for my parents not telling me the truth all those years. The birth certificate and the other stuff were my only leads."

He could tell she was determined not to cry, and he was a little surprised when she didn't. Instead, a tear slipped down Rose's cheek.

"You've proven the birth certificate is useless, so that probably means the other stuff is, as well. I'll probably never be able to explain why my mother had those things hidden away."

"I know a way you might be able to find the answers you want," Ian said.

Hannah flinched as if she'd been struck. "How?"

"By asking the right question."

"Which is?"

"Who has been following you?"

"How will that help me find my birth parents?" Hannah asked.

"Because whoever was driving that green car today didn't just follow you, Hannah. He tried to kill you. Might be helpful to know why."

Chapter Six

Hannah and Ian were served dinner in the privacy of the office. It was Rose's idea, which Ian was all for. They had to get Hannah's things from her motel and do another errand before they went to the condo.

Joleen had carried the tray up the stairs in one hand and was juggling a tray stand in the other. He immediately went to her aid. "Just tell me what to do," he said as he took the stand.

"Open it and I can put this tray down," Joleen answered with such gratitude that it made Ian wonder if it was possible that this quiet woman was unaccustomed to offers of assistance.

Once she had the tray in place, the room filled with wonderful aromas. Joleen fussed with a bud vase, centering the single white rose before she lifted the plate covers and revealed their meals.

"That isn't food, it's art!" he heard Hannah exclaim as she surveyed the beautiful presentation of fresh seafood, crisp, colorful vegetables and decorations of small onions and roasted potatoes in identical oval shapes. The plates were decorated with creative ribbons of sauces and sprinkled with some green herbs.

Without ever looking up, Joleen uncorked a bottle of wine and poured generous amounts of a fruit-scented white into two glasses. "If you need anything else," she said as she opened the cloth napkin to reveal a basket of warm, yeasty rolls, "press seven on the intercom." Joleen reached the door before she glanced back just long enough to say, "I hope you enjoy your dinner."

"How could we not enjoy this?" Hannah asked as she dragged a chair over to the makeshift table.

As appealing as the food was, it paled badly in comparison to Ian's companion. This was his first real opportunity to observe Hannah up close. He carried over a chair for himself and joined her. He wondered if she knew that her hair reflected the sunlight coming in through the window. Or that her face lit up like a child's as she lifted the glass of wine to her mouth. She stopped just shy of taking a sip.

"Is there a reason why you're staring at me?"

The question came out without accusation or reprimand. In fact, her soft, probably unintentional sensual tone robbed him of his appetite along with his sanity. His only real need at that instant was to know what it would be like to hold her in his arms and kiss her until his senses returned.

"I don't think you want to know," he answered with a sheepish grin.

To his surprise, she took a quick sip of wine, placed her glass on the table, rose and came close to him. She smelled of flowers and her pastel T-shirt left very little to his imagination. On any other woman, her pants would have been called jeans. On Hannah, they were a denim second skin, revealing the faint outline of her well-toned legs to his very curious eyes. Ian felt his pulse quicken, speeding up to match the urgency that seemed to be building in his gut with each passing second.

Because of the difference in their heights, he and Hannah were eye level for the first time. He watched as she took what appeared to be a fortifying breath before she said, "You're either going to like what I'm about to suggest, or I'm about to embarrass the hell out of us both."

Intrigued, Ian shifted so that she now stood just beyond the V-shaped opening of his legs. "I don't embarrass easily," he assured her. "Go for it."

That should have given her some sense of confidence, but it appeared as if she was growing more tense.

"Hannah?"

"Here goes," she said with rapid-fire quickness. "I know we've only known each other one day. We know virtually nothing about each other, but..."

"I think you were about to get to the good part," he said when she hesitated. He was pleased when she returned his smile.

"I'm not married."

Ian had not expected that, so he gave a little chuckle before saying, "Me, either." That seemed to come as a relief to the nervous beauty.

"I think you're an incredibly nice man. I know you didn't really want to stay here to help me."

"Hannah?" Ian reached out and captured her hands in his. Cautiously, he gave a gentle tug until she fit into the cradle of his opened thighs. He heard her swallow and purposefully moved one finger to her pulse point at her wrist. It was too fast to count. Whether it was just to save her from whatever she was finding so impossible to say, or whether he was just giving into his own selfish wants, Ian decided this was one situation that required action instead of words.

He leaned forward until his lips barely brushed hers. It was a calculated move, since he wasn't positive that his kiss would be welcomed. He was very, very wrong.

Shaking free from his hold, Hannah draped her arms around his neck and took the kiss from tentative to demanding in record time. Ian's hands gripped her small waist, then traveled upward, stopping at her rib cage with his thumbs just beneath the swell of her breasts. She responded by raking the fingers of her one hand through his hair as she moved closer, pressing into him. If she had any doubts that he was enjoying this unexpected encounter, they had to have been erased then. If he could feel the buckle of her belt, she could surely feel the stiffness she'd inspired.

Her tongue teased and moistened the seam of his lower lip. She tasted like wine and felt like heaven. Her hands mussed his hair before cupping his cheeks, holding him still. He didn't understand at first, then she ended the kiss but made no move to ease the closeness of their bodies.

Her face was flushed and her eyes were a sultry mixture of unspent passion and blatant need. Ian's attempt to get at her mouth met with resistance. Instead, Hannah took her thumb and ran the pad back and forth over his lip, creating heat and friction that was almost as enticing as having her pliant mouth. She watched what her actions were doing to him. She appeared almost mesmerized by him. "I thought that if we kissed, it might solve the problem."

"Problem?"

Slowly and more than just a little reluctantly, Hannah stepped away from him. "I thought that if we kissed each other and it turned out to be the horrible, awkward experience that first kisses usually are, then we could both stop thinking about it."

He pondered her hypothesis as she went back and took her seat. Waiting until he was certain his hand wouldn't shake, he took a long sip of wine. Using his most conversational tone, he asked, "Have you been thinking about kissing me?"

Hannah's fork hovered in midair as she met his eyes. "Yes. What about you?"

"I never kiss myself."

Her laughter seemed to quell some of the tension in the room. She was so beautiful when she smiled.

"I was asking if you had considered kissing me," she clarified before taking the food into her mouth.

Ian sighed theatrically. "Only about a billion times. And that's just counting when I was awake."

His answer should have pleased her; instead, her light eyebrows drew together in a frown. "I wish you would have told me that before I acted on my very-flawed theory."

"And your theory was?"

"That one or the other of us would find the experience repulsive so that we could simply be friends."

Ian laughed long and hard. "In general, men and women cannot be friends. Being more specific and a little graphic, after that small sample, the last thing I want from you is friendship."

From the doorway he heard Rose clear her throat, and he whipped his head around, knowing he had to look like a guilty little boy. "How long have you been standing there?" he demanded.

Rose's grin was wide and almost an answer in itself. "Long enough to feel the heat you two were putting out."

"Rose!" Hannah cried.

Ian glanced at his dinner companion, who was now the same shade of red as the shell of the lobster tail on her plate.

As reality returned, he blew out a breath and grabbed his fork as if it were a weapon, and began to eat. His mind was reeling from a raging battle between his pleasant memories of having Hannah in his arms and his guilt for feeling things he had no business feeling. Not with Carmen gone.

He had hoped Rose would take the hint and

leave them alone. Apparently, Rose didn't take hints. He was annoyed and Rose was convenient, so he angrily asked, "Is there a reason you're still here? If you're hanging around waiting to see if we'll give into the throes of passion on the area rug, you're wasting your time. What you witnessed was a fluke and a mistake." He saw the pain in Hannah's beautiful eyes, but he knew these things had to be said. "It won't *ever* happen again." He met Hannah's gaze and in a softer tone said, "It can't ever happen again."

AN HOUR LATER, Hannah was seated next to Ian in the car as they pulled onto the expressway. She was still wondering how Ian could have shared that kind of kiss with her, only to make a public announcement that it would never happen again. This wasn't normal rejection, she thought as they melded into the steady stream of early-evening traffic. She sensed he was as curious about her as she was about him, yet something was holding him back. Great! *I find a man that makes my toes curl and he has more baggage than a cargo carrier.*

Her observation was confirmed when she turned to take a quick look at his handsome profile. He'd worn that stony expression when he had abandoned her for nearly thirty minutes after dinner. Ian had returned, told her they would collect her things from the motel and he would take her to the condo. His single mention of the brief passion she thought they had shared was when he said, "We won't let what happened get in the way of finding out who wants to harm you. It was just a pretty ordinary kiss, so your theory was right.''

Ordinary kiss, her brain repeated sarcastically. Does he think I'm a fool? That kiss was mind numbing. She'd seen the desire in his eyes. What she didn't get was the reason why he was trying so hard to pretend otherwise. Well, she pondered in silence, it might be interesting to learn who he was trying to convince, and she had a hunch it wasn't her.

''Where are we going?'' she asked when he steered his Jeep off the highway.

''It's safer if we take back roads. If someone is tailing us, I should know soon enough.'' He could almost feel the tension begin to stiffen her small body. Battling to keep his attention on driving, Ian wondered if he should tell her about all the arrangements. *No,* his conscience piped up. What he should be doing is telling her the truth. But there was no way he could ever admit what he had done. Not now, not knowing how wonderful it had felt to have her in his arms. If she learned the truth about what he was, she would do what most of his other friends had done—contemptuously ignore him.

''Rose said the condo is furnished,'' he told her. ''And I'll wager it's a whole hell of a lot nicer than that place you were staying, I would imagine. How could you sleep with that red neon sign flashing on and off? And all that noise from the street!''

''Maybe I like noise. Not everyone shuns all things social,'' she said rather indignantly. ''You and Rose are only trying to help, and I appreciate it, but I'm not sure I'm ready to be locked away in the Ivory Condo on the chance that someone really is following me.'' By the time she finished, she was fairly screaming at him.

He let out a slow, calming breath. This woman's temper was the last thing he wanted to deal with. He was having a hard enough time dealing with his own guilt and frustrations. ''You're welcome to bring anything to the condo you want.''

''Gee, thanks,'' she retorted. ''Will I also be given a half hour of exercise in the yard?''

For some reason, her prison analogy struck him as funny and he laughed aloud, which didn't seem to sit too well with his companion. ''According to Rose, there's plenty of room,'' he said as he veered off on a side street into a tree-lined suburb. ''Incidentally,'' he began as he took a quick glance over his shoulder, ''did you leave anything back in New Orleans?''

''I took a six-month leave of absence,'' she said in defense of the two garment bags, three suitcases, a duffel bag on wheels and no less than three carry-on pieces. ''I'm sorry my packing doesn't meet with your approval. Perhaps I should call the local shelter and donate all my clothing and personal items. Would that wipe that snotty look off your face? Would that be penance enough for kissing you? Besides, sharing a kiss with you wasn't all that great for me, either.'' He could feel the warmth of her breath against his right ear as she spoke. ''And you were right about it not happening again. Not because you said so, but because *I* say so."

"Meaning?"

She was quiet for several minutes while Ian whipped the Jeep into one of the spots reserved for the unit number Rose had supplied. "What did you mean?" he asked again.

"I wasn't speaking in tongues," she snapped as an attentive doorman appeared and helped her down from the vehicle.

Ian stood scanning the gated entrance and the parking lot. He told himself that he was only doing a job. He didn't believe it, though. The dallying gave him time to work on the conflicting emotions churning in his gut. What with having Hannah announce that whatever they might have started at the Rose Tattoo was already finished. *Wasn't that exactly what I said in front of Rose? I should be thrilled that Hannah has decided she doesn't want me. This job won't be complicated by the two of us starting something that could only lead to disaster.*

"So why do I feel like I've been rejected?" he wondered aloud as he headed for the front door of the high rise. *Worse yet, why do I feel like I want to change her mind?*

THE DOORMAN DIRECTED HER to the office of Mrs. Wilkerson. She glanced back and saw Ian still in the parking lot as she entered the domain of the resident manager. Mrs. Wilkerson sported a tight bun atop her head, very conservative clothing and a pair of bifocals on a chain around her neck. She didn't smile, but then she had one of those sucking-on-a-lemon mouths and probably couldn't smile even if she tried. Hannah had the distinct impression that this woman never tried. Luckily, Mrs. Wilkerson's genes had given her a long, straight, pointy nose that she put to great use. She looked down it at Hannah as if she was some sort of undesirable that would require the office to be fumigated after their meeting.

Hannah decided the best way to deal with a snooty person like Mrs. Wilkerson was to kill her with kindness. So, donning her brightest smile, she said, "Nice to meet you," adding her full name and offering her hand. Mrs. Wilkerson accepted neither her warmth nor her extended hand. Awkwardly, Hannah took a seat at the same moment Ian joined them.

At that instant Hannah knew that the resident manager was some sort of Stepford Wife. It was the only way to explain her lack of reaction to a man as exceptionally handsome as Ian. Only a blind woman or a robot could ignore the kind of masculine appeal Ian exuded without effort.

"I received a fax from Mr. Porter this afternoon," Mrs. Wilkerson said at the same time as she reached her bony fingers into a drawer and retrieved a file. "While you have permission to use his unit, you must realize that the Porters have placed it on the market and our agreement states we can show the condominium whenever we choose." She handed Hannah several official-looking sheets of paper.

Hannah quickly read the sales agent agreement.

"We will make every reasonable effort to—"

"There's no need for you to explain," Hannah cut in as she rose. "I'm an attorney, and I am quite able to read this and adhere to the terms agreed to by you and the Porters."

Mrs. Wilkerson obviously didn't care for Hannah's reaction because her already puckered lips were pinched more tightly. "Fine," she snapped. "Here is a copy of the cleaning schedule, trash and recycling guidelines. If we get an offer acceptable to the Porters, you'll have to vacate the residence immediately, is that understood?"

"Yes," Ian answered. "We're expecting a Detective Dalton Ross this evening. Please see that he is shown up directly."

"A police officer?" Mrs. Wilkerson gasped, clutching her pencil-thin neck. "Should I prepare myself and the other residents for the type of shenanigans that went on when Mr. Porter lived here?"

Hannah watched as Ian gave the older woman his brightest smile, winked outlandishly, then said, "Naw, we'll probably be much worse than the Porters. C'mon, Hannah," he said as he tossed the keys to the unit in the air, then let them fall into his opened palm. "Have the doorman unload the Jeep while we go up and make sure the place is to our liking."

Mrs. Wilkerson looked on the verge of a case of the vapors. "This is a quiet place. Our residents adhere to a certain code of behavior that—"

"Don't worry," Ian said as he steered Hannah toward the door. "We only party on weekends and we always clean up after the animal sacrifices."

Miraculously, Hannah held her reaction until the elevator doors slid shut. Crumpling the list of dos and don'ts provided by the resident manager, she doubled over with laughter. "Good grief, Ian, if I hadn't known better, I'd have thought you were serious. Animal sacrifices?" She looked up into his smiling gray gaze. Other than the mischievous light in his eyes, he looked as innocent as a newborn babe.

The elevator opened to a hallway on the upper floor that was home to only two units. That was her first clue that she was way out of her socioeconomic bracket.

"Something tells me I couldn't afford the utilities for a place like this."

Ian, who was a stride ahead of her, stopped, blocking her path as he turned and looked down at her. "I thought you said you lived in the garden district in New Orleans?"

Hannah felt her lashes flutter against her cheeks as she avoided his probing eyes. "Aside from learning that my parents weren't my parents, I also learned that our house wasn't our house. The bank foreclosed before my parents' burial vault had been sealed."

"So that line you fed me in the car to explain your overabundance of luggage wasn't exactly true, was it?" he asked with kindness instead of the judgment she had braced herself for.

"I didn't lie exactly. I just omitted the fact that I'm temporarily homeless." Hannah sidestepped the tall man and went to the door and waited for him to unlock it. "I do have a job, Ian. It isn't like I'm going to live in a box over a grate begging passersby for spare change. I..."

Hannah fell silent when he pushed open the door and she got her first peek at her temporary new home. In her wildest dreams, Hannah could never have envisioned what she saw when she stepped into the spacious condo overlooking Charleston Harbor. The condo was ultracontemporary, all open spaces, stark white walls and white furniture. Hannah made a mental note not to allow Chad or Cassidy Tanner to pass over the threshold of this stunning but sanitary place.

"You don't like it," Hannah said when she turned and took in the deep frown lines at the corners of his mouth.

"What's not to like?" he answered blandly as Hannah moved to the double doors to take in the magnificent view of the water and the Charleston skyline beyond.

"It probably has a killer view at night and it should get dark in an hour or so," she murmured when she sensed him come up behind her. "I can even see Fort Sumter from here," she said, unable to quell the genuine enthusiasm she felt.

"Rose said it has a great kitchen," he said, his breath warm where it washed across the exposed skin of her neck.

Hannah felt her pulse quicken and knew it was imperative that she put some space between herself and Ian. The temptation of his closeness was nearly overwhelming. "Let's go take a look," she suggested, and she was careful not to make contact with his big body.

Rose was right. The kitchen had every modern convenience, including a built-in grill, a Sub-Zero refrigerator and a warming oven. ''This is almost better than the facilities back at the Rose Tattoo,'' she teased. ''Rose must have been blown away when she saw this.''

''Something tells me she'd be more impressed if this was Graceland,'' he teased.

Hannah met and held his silver eyes. They were mere inches apart and she felt drawn in spite of their joint proclamations that nothing more would happen. They continued in this look-but-don't-touch mode for several drawn-out moments. Hannah was neither conceited nor promiscuous, but she could certainly recognize that this man wanted her. Just as she wanted him.

She also remembered the humiliation of hearing him tell Rose the kiss they had shared meant nothing. Worse yet, that it had been a mistake, some lapse of judgment.

It was Ian who cut the thread of desire when he spun suddenly and started to explore the cabinets and appliances. She had a hard time believing that Ian the Recluse gave a flaming hoot about the latest modern conveniences. She was fairly sure his move was calculated to quash that intangible something that had left her with damp palms and a racing heart.

As he opened the refrigerator, Hannah had a completely unobstructed view of his tight derriere encased in well-worn denim. The outline of powerful thighs was clearly visible, as well. His shirt was the only thing nonwestern about him. In fact, that had been one of the first things she had noticed about him.

Her vision of a Montana rancher included a bolero tie, western-cut, chambray shirts and a dusty Stetson. Ian's only link to his secluded home seemed to be the snakeskin boots he wore. Without those, he could have been from just about anywhere.

"I'd like to see the rest of the place," she said. "I'll brace the door open so that poor doorman won't get a hernia when he brings up my things."

Ian took a step forward so that they were almost side by side. "I'll go with you, I need to learn my way around, too."

"Why?" she called out as she placed a heavy vase in a position to keep the door from closing.

Apparently, he opted to ignore her question. Ian led her down the hallway, opening the doors to a fully stocked linen closet and powder room along the way.

The next room they came upon was what she assumed was the master bedroom. "I guess this is yours," he told her, his eyes fixed on hers.

Hannah swallowed, then forced a smile to her lips. "This place obviously comes with a bedroom that doubles as a ballroom. This room has to be thirty feet by fifty feet. What did J.D. and Tory do with all this space? They probably used cell phones to carry on conversations." Her humor seemed to short-circuit the undercurrents of tension. Of course, the electricity came back on the instant she caught her first glimpse of the huge bed dominating the room. The mere thought of the combination of Ian, herself and a bed the size of a football field was enough to light the fire in the pit of her stomach. To keep from making the mistake of acting out her sudden-though-impossible desire to tackle him, toss him down on the comforter and rip his clothes off, Hannah averted her eyes, looking at what she could see of the bathroom.

"It comes with a pool, too," she joked as she moved to run her fingers along the smooth, cool tiles of the first step leading up to a deep, more-than-one-person Jacuzzi. Tilting her head back slightly, she grinned at his frown and asked, "What? Do the Jacuzzis at your hotel come with a diving board?"

"Cute," he murmured as he guided her back into the hallway. "This looks like an office," he remarked as he pushed open the next door and flipped a switch on the wall to combat the growing darkness of the descending dusk. "At least it has a daybed," he grumbled. "During the day maybe you can do some of Joanna's work from here."

"Who cares about the daybed? Wow," she gushed with excitement when she moved in to admire the state-of-the-art setup. The computer equipment was like something out of a science-fiction novel. "Does it have Internet setup?" she asked as she surveyed the different machines that formed a V and used up most of two walls. Hannah went to the computer and began to examine it.

"I'm sure it probably has the latest version," Ian remarked, reaching out to press the master switch of the control panel.

In no time she was treated to a full-color version of everything the computer had loaded. A lot of the programs had to do with computer-aided design for various buildings and structures. Then she recalled that J.D. was an architect and Tory did something in restoration.

"Wanna see what it can do?" Ian asked.

I'd much rather see what you can do, she thought. Luckily, she was in front of him, facing the screen, so he couldn't possibly read her uncharacteristically impure thoughts. "Sure." Her eyes were riveted to the screen as she sat in the padded rolling chair in front of the machine.

Ian reached around her, and Hannah felt the hardness of well-defined muscles press against her back. Her body felt alive where it touched his. The soft mat of dark hair on his forearms tickled as his large fingers worked nimbly on the keyboard. He had a scent all his own, heady and masculine—and it was almost as incredibly distracting as her surprise over his obvious mastery of the computer.

Hannah forced her attention upward to the image filling the screen. She didn't find it nearly as interesting as the gentle brush of his cheek against her earlobe. The room felt suddenly warm, a stark contrast to the clammy dampness of her palms as she flattened them against the front of her jeans.

Afraid she might leave huge, telltale sweaty palm prints on her clothing, she quickly jerked backward.

In the process, she managed to give Ian a decent whack in the jaw with the back of her head.

"Sorry," she said as complete humiliation vanquished desire. "Must have been a muscle spasm or something."

"No harm done," he said calmly and evenly before reaching around her and continuing his work.

Hannah squirmed in the chair as he showed her the various options and programs that she could access. Normally, she would have been captivated by the impressive power, speed and capability of the computer. However, normal didn't seem to apply where Ian was concerned. Not in the way she was so cognizant of the fluid motions of his body, the deep, soothing tone of his voice.

"How did a rancher get so computer literate?" she asked, pushing away from the computer and rolling over his foot in the process. "Oops."

"Now I know why they say most accidents happen in the home." He grunted as he hopped on one leg, rubbing his injured instep.

"I'm not usually this klutzy," she admitted, her eyes downcast. "I don't know what my problem is."

"Yes, you do, you just don't want to admit it." There was nothing but understanding in his tone. "If it's any consolation, I'm suffering from the same malady. I can't be close to you without wanting to hold you."

Never had she heard such kindness or honesty from a man before. It was in the deep blue-gray of his eyes, in the sexy half smile on his lips. However, what should have made her feel better only magnified her own awkwardness. Hannah was somehow conscious of herself in a whole new way. Things like posture, her hair, her wrinkled blouse. It all seemed to matter. All for a man who was willing to admit an attraction he was determined to ignore. But why? His expression yielded no clues, so she hoped a change in venue might help to clear her thoughts.

Wrapped in the warmth of the smile still curving his lips, Hannah and Ian made their way back to the kitchen. He directed her to one of the bar stools while he moved to the refrigerator.

After rummaging a bit, he appeared from behind the door with a bottle of wine. "I'm glad to see Rose stocked us with the necessities."

"Wine is a necessity?" she asked with mock exaggeration.

"Before I forget," Ian began as soon as he had uncorked the bottle, "there's one small detail that I think Rose left out when she insisted you move in here. I'm—"

Ian's sentence was silenced by the sound of the vase moving and the door hitting the metal stop. He gave her a wink, put the wine bottle on the counter and said, "Relax. I'll help the doorman with your worldly possessions. That way it will only take about an hour to unpack the Jeep."

"Very funny," she mocked at his back.

Hannah was still grinning when she heard a loud thud, then footsteps, then everything went black.

Chapter Seven

Using the sliver of light that shone beneath the door, Hannah scooted closer to Ian's still form. With her hands and ankles bound, it was no easy task, but she finally managed to place her cheek against his chest. Relief filled her when she heard the strong, regular beat of his heart.

The scent of industrial cleanser filled her nostrils. It was strong enough that even though some sort of tape covered her mouth, she could still taste the smell.

Then more than just light slipped under the door. Hannah went still and tried to make out the snippets of a male voice.

"...won't look like suicide...wasn't alone... but if she finds us..."

Her first instinct had been to go to the door and kick it in the hope that someone would hear her and come to her aid. However, the bits of conversation she had heard convinced her to rethink that idea. Whoever was on the other side of the door sounded more like foe than friend.

Nudging Ian proved useless, and part of her

was afraid that he might wake up and somehow alert their captor to the fact that they were no longer unconscious. Another part feared that he wouldn't wake up ever.

"Think!" she whispered as she urgently scanned the shadows of what she guessed was the janitor's closet. Once her eyes adjusted to the dim lighting, she spotted what she hoped would be her salvation. Ian still hadn't moved, and she worried—not for the first time—that his injury might be severe.

The floor was cold, rough, poured concrete and each time she rolled over a sharp spot, she grimaced, which in turn caused the tight tape over her mouth to pinch her skin. By the time she reached her goal, she was a mass of sweat, dirt and fear. Now comes the hard part, she thought as she braced her back against the metal edge of the shelving and wriggled her bound feet beneath her. She stopped once when a can of something fell with what sounded to her like a deafening clang. Hannah held her breath, certain their captor heard the noise. In the silence, she listened for his muffled voice or footsteps. She stayed that way until her thighs were screaming in agony from bearing the majority of her weight for such a long time in such an awkward position.

Finally, Hannah was standing and blindly using her fingertips to hunt for the protruding nail she had spied from the floor. When she finally succeeded, it was at the expense of a painful wound to her finger.

Once she had freed her wrists, she ripped the

tape from her mouth, stifling a scream. As tears filled her eyes, then fell down her cheeks, she removed the tape from her ankles and went to check on Ian.

Leaning close to his ear, she whispered his name as she gently patted his cheek. When he moaned, Hannah ripped the tape from his mouth, which brought him to full consciousness almost instantly.

"Wh—"

Hannah silenced him by placing her finger against his lips. "I heard him outside the door. I don't know if he's still there," she whispered.

Ian nodded, held out his wrists for her to remove the tape, then undid the binding on his ankles before he felt the back of his head. "What did he hit me with?" he asked softly.

"I never saw him," Hannah said. "One minute I was sitting on the bar stool, the next minute I woke up smelling cherry bathroom freshener in the dark."

She followed the outline of Ian's silhouette as he went over and pressed his ear against the door. He stayed there for what felt like forever before saying, "Something must have scared him off," he said in a normal tone. Hannah heard him jiggle the doorknob and waited for some evil man to come bursting in to kill them both.

When it didn't happen, she felt a little less scared and her brain started to function in a more normal, rational fashion. "We have to get out of here," she said.

"Duh," Ian said before he slammed his shoulder against the door. It made some noise, but it didn't open. He did it again, with the same results.

Hannah groped the air and found a string, gave it a yank, then smiled as the small room filled with light from a bare bulb. There was a trickle of blood on the back of the collar of Ian's shirt.

"You're hurt," she said as she came up behind him and parted his hair and found a nasty gash. "Instead of exerting all your strength on that door, why don't we just pick the lock?"

He turned, gave her an impatient look and said, "I don't have a lock-picking kit with me. They frown on stuff like that in airports."

Brushing aside his negative attitude, Hannah searched the room. "There has to be something in here we can use. Help me out, Ian. You were the secret agent, start *agenting*."

She heard him expel a breath as if to say her idea was nothing but a waste of time. Halfheartedly, he moved a few bottles of cleanser around while she climbed the precarious, wobbling shelves. Some of the things she came across smelled horrific, and her tears were now the result of harsh solvents, not emotion.

"You're going to break your neck," Ian observed with a twinge of annoyance. "Climb down from there before the thing pulls away from the wall and you get us both crushed."

Hannah turned, with the intention of telling him exactly what she thought of his lack of effort, when she saw it. She felt a slow smile come to her mouth as she remembered something that could free them.

"Give me your shirt and let me get on your shoulders," she said.

Ian was looking up at her as if she had just given him an order for pizza. "My shirt and my shoulders?"

An exasperated breath came out in a rush as she said, "I need to be on your shoulders so I can reach the lightbulb. I need your shirt because it's probably hot, and I don't want to burn myself."

Rather reluctantly, Ian pulled his shirt over his head and handed it up to her. For a split second, Hannah's brain registered short, dark hair covering his chest, then tapering to a thin line before it disappeared into the waistband of his jeans. When she climbed on his shoulders, her awareness of this man lasted much longer than a split second. His shoulders were broad and strong and she felt the ripple of his stomach muscles pressed against the backs of her legs as he guided her to the center of the room.

Tapping the bulb, she found it too hot. Wrapping her hand in his shirt, she carefully unscrewed the bulb, throwing them back into near-total darkness again.

"Just stay still," Ian instructed. "Don't wiggle around until you feel your feet on the ground."

"No problem," she said. She cradled the lightbulb as if it was a crown jewel. When Ian had her safely on the ground, Hannah went to the door and felt the knob until she found the small holes housing the lock mechanism.

"What are you doing?" Ian asked, clearly exasperated.

"I'm about to ruin your shirt, but it has blood on it anyway and that's so hard to get out."

"I was asking for a specific answer, not laundry tips," he said as she stepped on the bulb wrapped in his shirt with the utmost care. "You took the lightbulb just so you could break it?"

Cautiously, Hannah felt through the shards of glass until she found the filaments. "Have some faith," Hannah said. "I've seen this work before."

She spent several minutes manipulating the metal filaments inside the lock until she heard the click of release. Ian, who had done nothing but mock her the entire time, suddenly stepped in front of her as they opened the door.

It was a good thing, too. There was a man in the hallway with a gun pointed right at them.

He yelled, "Freeze!" but Hannah really didn't need the instruction. Just seeing the gun was enough to turn her body rigid with renewed fear.

"Ian MacPhearson?" the gunman asked.

Hannah was unceremoniously shoved behind Ian as he shielded her when she must have appeared unable to move under her own steam.

"Who wants to know?"

Hannah heard some rustling, then a snap, then he answered, "Detective Ross, Charleston, P.D."

Every molecule of adrenaline in her body seemed to seep out when she realized she wasn't going to die. She half fell, half leaned against Ian, who caught her and supported her with one arm. They remained in that position as they walked back down to where the condo door stood open.

The first thing Hannah noticed was that all of her luggage, as well as a few pieces she didn't recognize, were stacked in the living room. The second thing she saw was the contents of her purse had been scattered on the floor, along with what she guessed were things from Ian's wallet, since a brown, hand-tooled man's wallet lay nearby.

This detective wasn't what Hannah thought of when she imagined a police official. This man was tall, broad shouldered, with unruly hair that wasn't as long as Gabe Langston's but certainly couldn't adhere to any regulation. He had one of those angled faces that most women found attractive. As he dialed for an ambulance on his cellular phone over Ian's strong protests, Hannah found her eyes drawn to a worn photograph among the debris.

She took a step closer, careful not to disturb anything, just as Detective Ross had instructed. The picture was of Ian, slightly younger, dressed from head to toe in khaki, with his arm around a dark, exotic-looking woman. At first she thought the jungle backdrop was one of those photographer's murals, then she saw the bandage with the reddish stain on Ian's left forearm.

She turned and instantly found a ragged scar that was a perfect match to the injury depicted in the photo. When she looked at Ian, she felt as if she was looking into the eyes of a stranger. His lips were little more than a thin, angry line, and every muscle of his well-toned torso was tensed to match his tightly balled fists.

When Detective Ross finished his call, he shook his head and said, "Rose told me something about a hit and run. She didn't tell me it took place in J.D.'s high-priced condo."

Hannah smiled at his attempt at humor. "Why would he dump my purse and go through Ian's wallet, but then leave my suitcases alone?" she asked.

"He was interrupted," Ian answered. Then pointing to some patterns in the carpeting, he said, "My guess is the elevator came up—probably the doorman with the bags—so he dragged us into the janitor's closet until the coast was clear."

The detective nodded his approval. "He waits for the doorman to finish, then starts to search for something. Then something scared him off." Detective Ross appeared apologetic. "It could have been me. I did hear footsteps on the fire stairs when I first arrived. Either of you have any idea what this guy was after?"

"I have nothing of value," Hannah said. "I have the kind of jewelry that turns your finger green from oxidation."

"I think you'd better sit down, Mr. MacPhearson," the detective suggested. "You, too, Miss Bailey."

They each insisted everyone be on a first-name basis. Hannah and Ian each occupied an end of the sofa, while Dalton sat in a contemporary chair that didn't look comfortable but probably was. Dalton flipped out a pad and pen, then asked, "Did either one of you get a look at this guy?"

"No."

"No," Ian said. "I poked my head into the hall because I thought I heard the doorman and, the next thing I know, Hannah and I are taped and gagged in the closet."

"He was outside the closet for a while," Hannah added. "I heard him talking."

Dalton and Ian seemed a touch encouraged by her story. "Did you recognize his voice?" Ian asked.

She shook her head. "It was muffled and I could only make out bits and pieces. He said something about not being alone." Hannah paused as her mind replayed the memory. "No, first he said it wouldn't 'look like a suicide,' then he said something about not being 'alone.' Then there was a pause and I heard something like 'if she finds us' or maybe it was 'finds out,' it was really hard to hear through that solid metal door."

Dalton looked up from his pad and asked, "What kind of pause?"

Hannah thought for a moment. "Like he was on the phone. It had to be that, because I never heard another voice. Only the one man."

"But it was definitely a man? Could it have been the same man who followed you?"

She shrugged, uncertain, just as a team of paramedics came into the condo carrying what she though was a little too much equipment for a couple of bumps on the head.

They took Ian into the kitchen where the lighting was better, and a young man who smelled as if he'd overdone the spice cologne examined the small lump on Hannah's head as well as the cut on the tip of her finger.

She considered Ian's injuries the most severe, but all he got was a small bandage and an ice pack. Hannah's head injury didn't seem to concern the paramedics nearly as much as the cut on her finger.

After the EMTs huddled in consultation, Hannah was forced to submit to a tetanus shot before they even bothered to offer her a bandage. Now the only thing that hurt was her arm.

Dalton and Ian agreed that the condo should be treated as a crime scene, but they also agreed it should be a low-key treatment.

For the next two and a half hours, Hannah sat alone on the balcony while state-of-the-art freezing stuff was sprayed around to lift fingerprints without leaving the sanitary condo buried in a layer of black dust. There was also a photographer, who captured every inch of the condo on film.

Lights from ships in the distance twinkled like stars, and she made several girlish wishes, which she was woman enough to know wouldn't come true. Still, it passed the time.

Dalton came out and joined her, looking tired, which reminded her that it had to be well past midnight by now.

"You look like you want to ask me something," Hannah prompted after a few minutes of awkward silence.

"Ian mentioned some items you brought with you from New Orleans."

They discussed the fact that she wasn't certain she'd been followed. Then, Hannah told him all about the phony birth certificate, the newspaper clipping and, when she started to describe the Oyster Point Society pin, Ian appeared.

He had put on a shirt—sort of. It was over his shoulders, but not buttoned, so with each gentle breeze off the harbor, Hannah fought to keep her eyes from gaping at the beautiful display of flesh and muscle. She wondered how he had gotten to the Omni and back with a clean shirt so fast. There probably isn't much traffic this time of night, she reasoned.

"Was your father Oyster Point?" Dalton asked.

Hannah and Ian's eyes met. Then Ian said, "I'm sure Hannah will be able to answer your questions after she gets some rest."

Dalton looked troubled. "But none of the things she mentioned are in the inventory we took here tonight."

Hannah smiled. "I have the pin in a very safe place," she explained. "I left the birth certificate and the newspaper locked in the trunk of my car, which is parked at the Rose Tattoo."

"I'll go by there on the way home and get them. They'll be safe with me and I'd like a chance to read them," Dalton suggested.

Hannah just shrugged, then winced at the sore muscle she had from her shot. "The news clipping is public record—I could replace it by simply asking for a copy. Ian has already proven that my birth certificate is a fake, so..." Her voice trailed off since there wasn't a lot she could say about the apparently useless things she had brought with her to the city.

Dalton shook her hand and seemed to genuinely wish her well. He promised to arrange for a patrol car to pass by the building on the hour, then Ian offered to walk him to the door.

He was back shortly, with his hand outstretched. "I think you need a soak in the...pool and a decent night's sleep."

She grinned. "I'll bet it is relaxing to lie in that thing with those jets massaging you." She sighed as she stood. She realized then that Ian smelled of soap and, upon closer inspection, she noticed he had shaved and washed the blood from his hair. "You must have set some speed records getting cleaned up and back here in such a short time."

Ian led her into the living room, which was still a mess with their personal possessions all mingled. "I was about to tell you something when our mystery man came. I guess I got sidetracked when he locked us in the closet. By the way, where'd you learn that trick with the lightbulb?"

"'MacGyver.'"

"Is this a teacher, a friend—who is he?" Ian asked as she grabbed her purse and started picking her things off the floor.

"'MacGyver' isn't a who, he's a what. It's a show that was on about this guy who hated violence, so he got himself out of sticky situations by using his brain and whatever was handy."

Ian roared with laughter. "I have a fictional TV character to thank for our escape?" he asked.

His laughter died when he saw that Hannah was now holding the picture from the jungle. Though a million questions came to her lips, she didn't want to sound intrusive, so she forced her tone to be light and chatty as she said, "I take it this is from your secret-agent days."

"Yes," he said as he came over and took the picture from her. "Carmen was my partner."

Partner could have a lot of meanings, and while she wouldn't have minded in the least if he wanted to tell her, it was clear he wasn't going to volunteer anything more. Hannah clamped her mouth shut and kept her curiosity to herself.

After she had put everything back into some semblance of order, she turned to find that Ian was still in the same spot, still staring at the photograph.

"I'll just go and take a dip in the pool," she said, backing out of the room.

The pained look in his eyes when he lifted his dark head stopped her. "Why haven't you asked?"

Hannah gave a half shrug. "One—it's none of my business. And two—something tells me I don't want to hear whatever you might say." She gave him a weak smile. "Just lock the door when you leave."

His expression became distant, as if he had transported himself back in time. Hannah was about to slip away when his eyes burned into hers.

"I've already locked and bolted the door, but I'm staying on this side of it."

"Excuse me?"

"Rose and I agreed that you'd be safer if I stayed with you."

Stunned and angry that she hadn't even been consulted, she said, "I don't need you to stay with me."

He tilted his head and gave her a mocking look. "Tonight didn't convince you that you're on someone's hit list?"

"Didn't tonight convince you that I'm not helpless? I'm the one that got us out of that closet, and you're supposed to be the hotshot agent. Instead of getting yourself locked in a broom closet, couldn't you have used some of your trained-to-kill skills?"

His eyes narrowed and there was the slight twitch of a muscle in his jaw. "Sorry to disappoint you, Hannah, but I gave up killing right after I killed my wife."

Chapter Eight

He's a killer. There is nothing but a wall separating me and a man who just confessed to being a killer.

Hannah paced back and forth at the foot of the huge bed. Ian had dropped his little bombshell, then locked himself in the office without further explanation. She walked to the dresser and spoke softly to her reflection in the mirror. "How did I get into this mess? I'm a bright, educated woman, who didn't want anything more than to find my biological parents. It's been less than three months since I lost my parents—who weren't my parents."

She watched herself frown. "Yes, they were your parents, Hannah. In every way that counted," she chided.

Spinning on the balls of her feet, she let out a breath as she leaned against the edge of the dresser, trying to gather her thoughts into something logical and cohesive. "Okay," she said with a sigh. "What do I know for certain?"

Ian MacPhearson is a killer.

Hannah pressed her fingers against her temples. "Forget that for now!" She spent several minutes with various unpleasant images of Ian flashing across her mind. She pictured him with a gun, a knife and then her brain played a silent version of Ian using his bare hands to strangle the life out of the woman in the photograph. It was nearly impossible to believe that the Ian she knew was capable of doing any of the horrible things her imagination had suggested. Hannah shoved her hair away from her face, shaking her head with disgust in the process.

The truth was, she didn't know him. Circumstance, along with a little help from Rose Porter, were the only reasons she even knew Ian MacPhearson was on this planet. It wasn't as if they had a relationship. So they shared one dinner and one kiss. She should have been leaping with joy that he had confessed before things had gotten...

She whirled around and gave herself an angry glare. "Gotten what? I'm acting as if I've learned a deep, dark secret about my one-and-only true love. Geez! I'm acting like an idiot," she muttered. "Transference," she decided after a short pause. "My feelings must be out of whack because I'm transferring my anger over my adoption being kept from me." She began to feel better. "Learning that Ian isn't what I thought he was is so close to learning that my parents weren't who I thought they were, and that's the only rational explanation for why I'm so upset. Ian is nothing more than a blip on the screen of my life, so my feelings of betrayal can't really be about him."

She moved toward the bathroom, pleased that she had worked things out in her mind. Now all she had to do was figure out a way to get Ian out of her life. Knowing she would figure some way to accomplish that by morning should have made her feel relief. Instead, as she peeled off her tattered and dirty clothing, she felt sad again. Not the kind of sad that comes at the end of a movie or the bittersweet conclusions of her favorite novels. This was the kind of sadness that made tears impossible. It wasn't as bad as what she had experienced when her parents had died, but it was similar enough for Hannah to feel the numbness engulfing her emotions as she stepped into the large tub. Contrary to what her well-intentioned friends had said, it wasn't easier for her to talk about her feelings. It was easier to just not feel.

"WHERE DO YOU THINK you're going?" Ian thundered when she walked into the kitchen with her purse in her hand.

"I called a cab from the bedroom," she explained in an even tone as she refused to make eye contact. "I'm going to try to catch Joanna and Gabe before their flight leaves." She might have avoided direct eye contact, but her peripheral vision was twenty-twenty. The scent of coffee mingled with the scent of soap as she passed Ian.

"Why?"

Hannah knew the best thing to do was ignore him. Just overlook the fact that he was leaning against the opposite side of the countertop, holding a mug with both hands, his shirt open and fluttering in the wake of her movement.

She didn't want to notice things like that, she reminded herself as she poured some coffee. She was too tired and it was too early in the morning. That was the only reason she would care that the top button of his jeans had been left undone. Or that his hair was a shade darker because it was still damp from a shower. Or that he hadn't yet shaved and the faint stubble made him even more attractive.

"I asked you a question," he said, though this time his tone was a bit more reasonable.

"I've changed my mind," she said, but she didn't turn around. "I'm no longer interested in finding a mother and father who gave me away."

"Is it because of what I told you?"

Fortifying herself with a sip of coffee, she turned and met his eyes. Hannah quietly studied his tired features but refused to alter her resolve. "Partly," she admitted.

"I guess I should explain. Carmen and—"

Hannah silenced him by raising her hand. "Don't. It's irrelevant, and in my line of work, I've heard every conceivable reason to justify murder so, unfortunately, whatever your reason, I'm sure I've heard it before. I've probably even written the kind of brief that kept you out of prison."

His lips clamped together into a tight, straight line, confirming her supposition that he was no different from the male and female felons her firm represented.

Hannah lowered her eyes to the shiny ceramic tile that reflected his image. "Andrew and Claudia Bailey were wonderful parents. Coming here was not only a mistake, it's dangerous. I'd rather go back to New Orleans than stay in Charleston with some lunatic following me around."

He crossed his arms in front of his chest. "What makes you think the guy who tossed us in the closet won't follow you back to New Orleans to finish the job?"

Hannah felt a shiver dance the full length of her spine. "I don't," she admitted. "But nothing bad ever happened to me in New Orleans. I'm hoping that will still hold true."

"I'm hoping you aren't that naive," he grumbled as the intercom buzzer sounded.

Hannah promised the doorman she would be right down for the waiting cab. From a safe distance, she extended her hand to him and said, "Thanks for offering to help. After I explain things to Joanna and Gabe, I'll send someone for my things." When Ian made no move to accept her hand, she let it fall to her side. "Well, then—" she took a last swallow of coffee and placed the cup in the sink "—goodbye."

He said nothing, at least nothing until she had closed the door. Then she heard a muffled string of curses. It wasn't until the elevator doors had closed that Hannah let out the breath she hadn't realized she'd been holding following the awkward scene.

Even with the doorman as an escort, she found herself looking around as a healthy dose of fear followed her from the building. After making sure that the photograph on the license and the cab-driver were one and the same, she gave the address for Joanna's office.

It was too early for rush hour, so it took Hannah less than ten minutes to realize that a red car was following them. To confirm her hunch, she gave the driver instructions to turn at the next corner. The red car followed.

Again Hannah gave a spontaneous instruction to the driver, and again the red car followed.

"Take me back to the condo," she demanded urgently as she battled to keep the panic from overtaking her.

"Forget something?" the driver asked, obviously annoyed.

"Just take me back," Hannah insisted as she pulled a twenty from her wallet and dangled it over his shoulder. It might be a different car, but she was terrified that there would be another attempt on her life. If she tried to explain things to the already fed-up driver, he might just dump her on the side of the road. "Please hurry," she urged in the best helpless-female tone she could muster.

The red car followed them all the way to the security gate, always staying just far enough back so that Hannah could discern only that the license plate was South Carolina issue and it had some sort of seal on it. The driver was nothing more than a dark, ominous silhouette behind the wheel.

It felt like an eternity before the cabbie brought the car to an abrupt halt in front of the building. He was surprised when she told him she wasn't going to need his services, and it cost her another twenty dollars on top of the fare to get the surly man to agree to stay at the front of the building until she was safely inside the elevator.

The doorman didn't seem surprised to see her, but it was probably part of his job description to smile blandly as he ushered her inside the elevator.

Ian didn't have a job description, yet she found him waiting for her in the hallway wearing a kind of relieved smile that quickly melded into a smug, superior smirk, which wasn't exactly what she needed at that instant.

"Don't get the wrong idea," she warned. "I only came back because—"

"Someone followed you," Ian finished for her. "I had a hunch we hadn't seen the last of our friend."

Hannah halted her march toward the penthouse, turned and was nearly bowled over by him. He grabbed her arms, steadying her after his much larger body had bumped her off balance. His eyes searched her face as his warm breath caressed her cheeks. "You're shaking." He ran his hands along her arms. The warmth of his touch and the genuine concern she saw in his gaze was almost enough to calm her frazzled nerves.

"I didn't think he'd be out there. Not once the police got involved," Hannah said. Reluctantly, she stepped out of his grasp and went into the condo. She sensed him behind her and wished she would have devised a contingency plan.

"We should call Dalton Ross," he suggested,

then grabbed the telephone. "Hopefully the cops will post a guard at the gate until I find out who is so interested in you."

"Whoa!" Hannah said as she fairly ripped the phone out of his hand. "Maybe I wasn't clear earlier. I've lived thirty-one years without knowing who my biological parents are, and no one ever followed me before. I think the best thing is to just go home and put this behind me."

His expression went from concerned to annoyed in a flash. "You aren't stupid enough to think you can walk away now. For all we know, the guy might think you can identify him as the guy who assaulted us last night and, in that case, he probably won't care if you're in Charleston or Antarctica when he makes his move."

"You aren't exactly putting my fears at ease," she snapped.

"You should have known better, Hannah. Or do you expect me to believe that what happened here last night simply slipped your mind?"

"This from the king of selective memory?" she retorted. "You are a master at letting people think you're one thing when you aren't."

He took the receiver back and rammed it down onto the cradle. "Meaning?"

"I'll bet Joanna and Gabe don't know about you. Or Rose. Or Shelby. Or Dylan."

She watched as the tiny muscles near his mouth twitched. It was only then that she realized the lunacy of what she was doing. The man was a killer and she was basically goading him into an argument. *Did I leave my brain in the taxi?* she wondered as she turned and dashed for the sanctuary of the bedroom.

She got maybe three feet before Ian grabbed her around the waist and carried her into the living room, deposited her on the sofa and glared down at her as if to dare her to try to move.

Hannah didn't move. Not when she looked up into the glistening slits of his narrowed eyes. Besides, having a physical confrontation with a man who was twice her size as well as a confessed killer didn't jibe with what she had learned at her YWCA self-defense class.

Apparently, her submissive front worked, because Ian took a few steps back and began to wring his hands as if he wasn't certain of his next move. Hannah was still trying to decide if that was good or bad, when he mumbled something unintelligible, rammed his fists into the front pockets of his jeans and fell into the ultramodern chair on the opposite side of the room.

Running was an option, though she was fairly certain that, despite his size, he'd get to her before she got to the door. There was a phone extension just inches from her fingers, but she couldn't picture him sitting idly by while she called for help. But she couldn't stand there waiting, either.

"If you have something to say, say it."

Whether it was the directness of her tone or the actual words themselves, she never knew. She only knew that Ian seemed to suddenly remember the past few minutes. The anger vanished and his features were a palette of apology and embarrassment. "I didn't hurt you, did I?"

"No."

"I have never done that to a woman before."

She considered his statement and the fact that he no longer had that angry, haunted look in his eyes, and some of her own emotions surfaced. "I guess it should be some comfort to know that you are a chivalrous killer. It's really not working for me, though, Ian. Call me conventional, but I find it a bit irritating to be hauled through an apartment—which is supposed to be some sort of safe haven—when I came here because some *other* weirdo was chasing me around Charleston at dawn."

Her sarcasm amused him. She could tell he was trying his best to keep from smiling.

"Is this funny to you?"

He held up his hands as he shook his head, but his grin didn't exactly come off as repentant. "I've just never been called a weirdo before."

Hannah blew out a frustrated breath. "I'd apologize, but I thought weirdo was a kinder word than murderer."

Ian sobered instantly. "I think we need to clear the air on that issue."

Her head fell back against the plush cushion as her eyes fixed on the paddles of the ceiling fan. "I honestly don't want to hear why or how or any of the excuses."

"I never said I had an excuse."

Hannah met his somber eyes and the pain she so easily recognized was almost enough for her to forget what he was. The instinct to go to him, to offer comfort, as her friends had tried to do for her, was very powerful, but she resisted by repeating the word *killer* in her mind. "Well, that is something," she told him, careful to keep her tone even and void of emotion. "Since you aren't in prison, I'll guess you either had a good attorney or a lousy prosecutor."

He raked one hand through his now-dry hair. "Neither, actually."

Despite her intellect reminding her it didn't matter, Hannah heard herself ask, "What happened?"

Ian stood and went to the French doors, shoving aside the curtain so that bright streams of yellow sunlight turned the white room a brilliant gold. It made the place seem surreal, as if she was some sort of princess holding court in a lavish, gilded room.

In a manner of speaking, she was. After six years of writing legal briefs, mostly arguing on the side of a convicted criminal, there wasn't much she hadn't seen or even invented herself when it involved the act of murder. The only thing that made this different was that Ian wasn't some name on a file, and there wasn't a senior partner telling her what to do. Ian was asking her to be judge and jury, and suddenly she didn't want any part of it.

"Never mind," she said as she leapt from the sofa. "It isn't like you owe me an explanation. It isn't like—"

"You're the first woman I've kissed in five years."

He couldn't have shut her up faster if he'd

stuffed a sock in her mouth. Men with perfect features, incredible bodies *and* intelligence were about as rare as their female counterparts. She was frustrated, intrigued and wished to hell he would lift his head so she could see his face.

"I'll assume that's because you live in the wilderness and there aren't any females," Hannah said. "I'd believe a man like you couldn't get a date about as much as I'd believe cell phones cause cancer and sitting too close to the television will make you go blind."

He laughed as he met her gaze. "I think I'm supposed to thank you for something in there. What did you mean by 'a man like me'?"

Hannah rolled her eyes. "I guess Montana doesn't have women or mirrors. Maybe the Red Cross can send some aid."

"Then that was an admission that you think I'm attractive?"

"Oh, please, Ian! We both know you're attractive, and I'd bet my last dollar that you've known it since puberty."

She actually watched his cheeks take on a pinkish tint. "Thank you and let's change the subject."

Hannah found his easy smile infectious. "Deal, so long as you'll answer one question first."

He hesitated, then said, "Maybe. Let's hear the question first."

Hannah laughed. "And people say lawyers are evasive."

"Hey," Ian began in his own defense, "I'm never sure what will come out of your mouth.

You aren't exactly shy about saying what you think."

"Daddy always considered that a lovely trait. My mother always cited it as the reason I am an old maid." Hannah did a perfect imitation of her late mother's well-intentioned put-down.

"Thirty-one is hardly old," Ian told her. "Maid is not a word I would use in the same sentence when describing you. I have a housekeeper back home. She's as wide as she is tall, and about the only trait the two of you share is that Phyllis doesn't couch her opinions, either."

"Why do you need a housekeeper if you never venture off your property?"

He came over and sat on the arm of the sofa, bringing them close to eye level since she remained standing. Hannah liked the position—it somehow made him less of a threat.

"I tried it solo for about six months and it was a disaster. I was so used to living in hotels that I didn't realize how tough it was until I was faced with things like laundry and grocery shopping."

Hannah took a deep breath before she blurted out, "And when you weren't in hotels, your wife did all those things for you?"

She dug her nails into her palms, waiting to see his reaction to her mention of his wife. She was fully prepared to watch those beautiful blue eyes turn into gray storm clouds. Instead, he surprised her by simply shaking his head. The motion was slow, almost mechanical. Hannah recalled experiencing that same numb stiffness in her own movements on the day she had buried her parents.

"Sorry," she mumbled. "Maybe we should agree that your past and your looks are both topics we won't discuss."

He shook his head vehemently. "No way. In fact, I want—no, make that *need*—to tell you what happened."

Without thinking about it, Hannah reached out and rested her hand on his broad shoulder, giving a gentle squeeze. "It isn't necessary, Ian. I'm not sticking around, so you certainly don't need to explain anything to me, since I'm sure we'll never see each other again."

When his hand covered hers, Hannah felt something totally unexpected. It wasn't like the electrifying jolt of their previous encounters. This was something far more intense. This was gentle and tender, and when their eyes locked, Hannah felt something intimate pass between them.

"I really want to tell you about Carmen, especially after last night."

She smiled. "I guess being unconscious and locked in a closet together does make us more than simple acquaintances."

He returned her smile. She wondered how a mere smile from this man was enough to cause a fluttering in her stomach. She wondered why he intrigued her with his volatile temperament and emotional baggage. She wondered how she could feel so drawn to a total stranger who was also a confessed murderer. She wondered why she hadn't left.

She knew the answers the instant he reached for her other hand. Ian MacPhearson possessed something intangible that drew her like a magnet. It was so strong that she could almost classify it as physical, yet he'd done nothing more than guide her to the seat next to him. Her hands had disappeared in his gentle grip. His eyes seemed heavy lidded as he held her gaze. He looked like a man with the weight of the world on his shoulders.

"I suppose the closet incident was a...*bonding* experience," he drawled. "But I was referring to the way I felt when we kissed."

Feeling the heat rush to her face, Hannah dropped her eyes and hoped to distract herself by focusing on the buttons of his shirt. *Big mistake. Huge mistake,* she corrected. Resplendent flashes of the memory of his bare chest only made her blush worse. She was definitely in the throes of some sort of mental disorder. That was the only explanation for her brain's sudden and vivid images of running her fingernails through the soft hair that covered the hard muscle of his chest. A complete personality break was the only plausible reason she would be thinking about such things when she should have been concentrating on getting as far away from Ian as possible.

His thumb hooked beneath her chin, forcing her to lift her face to him. His expression wasn't mocking or nasty as he scanned what she knew was her flaming red face. *Thank God he can't read my mind!*

"I guess I'll always know where I stand with you," he said softly. "Believe me, it's taking every ounce of my control to keep from giving in to my very strong desire for you, too.''

Hannah winced. ''I don't think I like the fact that you can finish my sentences and read my mind.''

He offered a playful wink. ''I wasn't reading your mind, just your body language.''

''Then I wish I knew how to tell my body to shut up,'' she muttered under her breath.

''It is one of your most attractive qualities,'' he assured her.

Hannah ripped her hands from his and brought them up to cover her face. ''This discussion is making me feel like a total fool.''

Pulling her hands back into his, Ian brought her palm to his lips and brushed a kiss against a sensitive spot she hadn't even known she had. As he brought her other hand close to the warmth of his mouth, he whispered, ''I have a feeling you're a lot of things, but a fool isn't one of them.''

Hannah was slow to respond. Actually, she silently acknowledged that she had responded, but not to his words. If he was telling the truth and he could read her body language, then she was in deep, deep trouble. ''You wanted to talk about your wife?''

Apparently, the *W* word was all it took to steer him back on track. He dropped her hands and sat more rigidly. She smugly decided that he wasn't the only one who could read body language.

''Aside from Gabe and a few other people I thought were close friends, I haven't discussed Carmen with anyone in years.''

"I don't think we know each other well enough for me to fall in the close-friend category," Hannah said. "You really don't have to tell me anything."

He didn't move, but Hannah sensed him growing distant. "Carmen and I were both Agency. We worked together in South and Central America mostly."

"There are some very unstable and dangerous places there," Hannah said when several minutes passed and Ian hadn't continued.

He blinked, as if he only then remembered that he had spoken aloud. "We had worked deep cover together for a couple of years, then we got married."

Hannah didn't miss the fact that he skipped over their courtship. "I would imagine two people could grow close working together like that."

"Partners do get close. Carmen was a beautiful woman."

"Yes, she was. I saw her picture."

Ian rubbed his jaw before speaking again. "We'd been working a mid-level drug dealer for the better part of a year before he agreed to make the introductions to his supplier. If I hadn't been distracted the night of the meeting, Carmen would still be alive."

"She was killed on the job? *By someone else?*"

"I didn't pull the trigger, but I'm still responsible."

"How can you say that?" Hannah demanded through her relief.

Ian grunted with self-disgust. "I didn't argue

when the middle man insisted that Carmen meet with his boss alone. I should have known that she'd been made."

Hannah gaped at him, then asked, "How?"

"Because of our cover. The way we set it up, Carmen was supposed to be a local, and I was her big American buyer. If I would have had my head screwed on straight that night, I would have called it off. Instead, Carmen was killed while I listened from a van parked a hundred yards away."

"So you've spent the past five years of your life in seclusion because you feel responsible for something you would have had to have been psychic to prevent?"

"We weren't rank amateurs, Hannah. Every agent who has listened to the tape from the wire agrees that Carmen's death was my fault. I became an instant pariah...so early retirement seemed...prudent."

"Sounds to me like they were being overly harsh and you only validated their stupid conclusions by retiring, especially if you were as good as Dylan said you were. Those other agents weren't there, and I find it very hard to believe that a smart guy like you would waste five years drowning in misplaced guilt."

"It wasn't misplaced."

Hannah took his hand and pressed it to her chest. "Yes, it was and it is. Unfortunately, the bad guys win sometimes. That's the way it works in real life."

"I was close enough. I could have gotten to her before the thing went sour."

"And probably gotten yourself killed in the process," Hannah argued. "I don't see a big red *S* on your chest. You aren't Superman, Ian. I'm sure you did all you could under the circumstances."

He gave a weak smile. "You sound like Gabe."

"No, I sound like an impartial person, listening to what happened without emotion, and all I've heard was that a slimy drug dealer killed an undercover agent who happened to be your wife. I hear something tragic and sad. I haven't heard anything that would make me think you were responsible for what happened."

"We had an argument that afternoon."

Hannah felt her heart ache. She would be eternally grateful for the fact that her last words to her parents had been loving. "I'm sorry, Ian, but there's no way you could have known that she'd be killed and you wouldn't have the chance to work things out."

"Really? Well, the last thing I said to Carmen before she went into that building was that I wanted a divorce."

Chapter Nine

Joleen approached the table where Hannah was having an early lunch with Rose and Shelby.

"This is from Tammy," Joleen said as she slipped a small sheet of paper onto the table. "She said you have an appointment with a client at three."

The shy, submissive woman was gone before Hannah even had an opportunity to thank her. "Is she always so quiet?"

Rose snorted. "She's been like this for a couple of days. Not that Joleen was ever what you might call a conversationalist."

"She works very hard," Shelby injected.

Hannah was beginning to sense that Shelby was one of those rare people that lived the cliché about if you can't say something nice about a person, say nothing at all. Rose, on the other hand, seemed ready, willing and able to say exactly what was on her mind. So, figuring she'd get the entire truth from Rose, Hannah directed her question to her. "Are you two baby-sitting me?"

Shelby's eyelashes fluttered as she toyed with the grilled chicken on her plate.

Rose unabashedly grinned. "Of course. Ian figured you'd be safe here, and it isn't like you know a lot of folks here in the city."

That was true, but it was still a bit humiliating to be dropped off at the Rose Tattoo as if it was some sort of adult day-care facility. "Detective Ross is making arrangements for a police guard at the condo," Hannah said.

Rose laughed. "I'll bet that scrawny old biddy Mrs. Wilkerson is thrilled having the cops in her parking lot."

Hannah chuckled, though she did feel a tad guilty for causing such a ruckus. Still, it was hard to feel too badly when she remembered the resident manager calling both her and Ian the type of unsavory elements that were not normally welcome at the prestigious address.

"I still think it would be best if I just went home," she said with a sigh.

"Nonsense," Rose scoffed. "When you have some lunatic after you, it doesn't matter where you go, they follow right along. My daughter-in-law had some creep stalking her. Believe me, you want to get this over and done with so you don't have to spend the rest of your life looking over your shoulder."

Hannah shivered at that unpleasant thought. "I don't even want to think along those lines! But for the life of me, I can't fathom why anyone would want to hurt me."

"Maybe it has something to do with Ian,"

Shelby suggested. "My husband said Ian has probably made more than his fair share of enemies, and the two of you *did* arrive on the same day."

"We should know shortly," Rose announced. "Ian's off meeting some guy to check on that possibility."

Hannah frowned. "How do you know that?"

"I asked," she answered proudly. "I figured if he wanted me to keep an eye on you, I should know where to reach him in case of any trouble."

Hannah's appetite died when she heard that. "I wish he wouldn't say things like that. It's getting to the point where he's got me afraid of my own shadow."

Shelby patted her hand. "You're safe here with us."

"Why are you doing this?" Hannah blurted out. "I mean, I appreciate the lunch, but Ian already proved that the birth certificate is garbage."

"Garbage with my name on it," Rose said huffily. "The last time somebody impersonated me, I ended up on trial for murder."

"That must have been terrible," Hannah said. "At least the system worked and you didn't go to prison."

Rose's green eyes shone with genuine anger. "None of this would have happened if Joe Don would have stayed at home like he should have. When I think about the lines he was feeding me when he showed up here pretending to want me back, I almost feel like digging him up and killing him for real."

"Thank heavens it all worked out," Shelby offered, along with a genuine smile that seemed to hint that beneath the grayish pallor due to her pregnancy, she was an exceptionally pretty woman. Then she turned to Hannah and added, "And I'm sure everything will work out for you, as well."

Hannah glanced back and forth between the highly contrasting women. "That still doesn't explain why you're willing to help me. It wasn't like I made a good first impression."

That made Rose laugh. "I will say, I haven't had a shock like that since Gabe told me he was my son."

"You had no idea?" Hannah asked. "You didn't sense that he was your own child?"

"Not a clue," she admitted. "Now I see the similarities between Gabe and J.D., but at the time I never suspected a thing."

Placing her fork down next to the plate of half-eaten food, Hannah leaned back in her chair. "There has to be a connection between you and my biological mother," Hannah said. "Do you remember a friend, a co-worker, anyone close to you back then that might be my mother?"

"I've been thinking about that," Rose said. "Waiting tables and tending bar, you meet a lot of people. A few of the girls got pregnant, but they were all married, and I still get Christmas cards or run into them around town. Sorry."

"What about Magnolia Gardens?" Hannah asked at the same moment Ian entered the restaurant.

He strode through the room and Hannah noticed that he got more than his fair share of attention from the female patrons. It wasn't just the fluid way his large body moved, or that his western-style clothing was rather unusual. Ian possessed a presence that demanded attention, and Hannah wasn't immune to it. In fact, quite the opposite was true, since she knew what it was like to be in his arms, knew the incredible power of his kiss.

Shelby greeted him before hurrying away from the table. Rose smiled at him as he pulled out the chair next to Hannah and joined them.

As Ian returned the greeting, his eyes remained fixed on Hannah, making her feel an odd mixture of flattered and embarrassed as she breathed in his unique scent.

Taking a grape from Hannah's plate, he popped it into his mouth. She told herself that he was just hungry; still, she couldn't quite seem to get past the feeling that his simple act conveyed a form of intimacy. Apparently, she wasn't the only one who read something into his action.

Rose was grinning like the Cheshire cat. "You two must have been busy last night. Did the two of you pick up where you left off at dinner? What *exactly* happened when you were locked inside that closet?"

"Rose!" Hannah gasped.

"A gentleman never tells," Ian said as he gave Hannah a lascivious wink.

Rose shook her head. "I hate gentlemen, they never seem to want to share the good stuff."

Thankfully, Joleen appeared at their table. She stood between Hannah and Ian as she took his order. Her perfume was familiar to Hannah, but, as was her practice, the waitress dashed off before she had an opportunity to comment.

Ian scooted his chair back to accommodate his height. In the process, his leg brushed hers, and Hannah had to concentrate hard to keep from reacting to the tantalizing sensation that began where he had touched her, then seeped into every cell until it finally settled as a knot in her stomach.

"My friend checked the list, and none of my former targets are known to be in the area."

Pushing her plate away, Hannah asked, "But does that mean there might be the possibility that this is about you and not me?"

He shook his head with finality. "Not after all this time. I've been out of the game too long."

Hannah sighed in frustration, then turned to Rose and restated her earlier question. "What about Magnolia Gardens?"

"What's Magnolia Gardens?" Ian asked.

"It's a popular tourist attraction out on Highway 61," Rose supplied. "What do you want to know about it, Hannah?"

Hannah laced her fingers and rested her chin against them. "My parents used to take me there a couple of times a year when I was little." Reluctantly, she shifted her attention to Rose and asked, "Did you ever work there?"

Rose chuckled. "Nope. They have a pretty upscale tea room. I've always been more comfortable with the beer-and-nuts crowd than the tea-and-biscuit crowd.''

''Somebody put your name on that birth certificate, Rose. Someone who knew you and Hannah's mother,'' Ian said. He shifted, locking his gaze on Hannah. ''What do you remember about those trips?''

She concentrated for several minutes. ''It was a long time ago. All I really remember is being bored.''

''Why?'' Ian asked.

''Because I was only four or five at the time, and I didn't like sitting on those benches.''

''You just sat on benches?'' he pressed.

''I was a little kid,'' she said defensively. ''I'm sure we did more than that, but I only remember sitting in the garden.''

Joleen delivered Ian's food and informed Rose that there was a pressing problem with a delivery, and Shelby had already gone home because she was ill again.

Before she left, Rose said, ''I hope you find this person soon. And she'd better have a damn good reason for using my name.''

Joleen, head bowed, asked if there was anything else she could do for them. Ian looked at Hannah, and once she indicated she was fine, Joleen moved on to the table next to theirs.

''I think we should drop in on the Oyster Point Society next,'' Ian suggested before he began to eat. He swallowed, then added, ''Maybe you should go into the ladies' room and get the lapel pin out of your bra before we leave.'' He grinned devilishly. "Or, you can wait until we're in the car. I'd be happy to—"

"How did you know?" she asked as she felt her cheeks warm. "I never said—"

"I felt it when I kissed you. I felt every inch of you when you were in my arms. I felt the soft fullness of—"

She held up her hand, "Okay, I get the picture."

His soft laughter followed her into the ladies' room. Once she had retrieved the pin, she remained by the vanity, fanning her face with a paper towel. There was no way she was walking back out there until her blush was gone and her heart was no longer pounding in her chest. Before exiting, she vowed she would get even with him.

HE SHOULD HAVE BEEN accustomed to being around her by now, but should and reality were two completely different things. He felt like a teenager as he watched her come toward him. Nothing slipped his notice. It was the first time he had seen her in a skirt, and he had to admit her legs were even better than they had been in his fantasies. The hemline just grazed her knee, revealing calves that were slender and toned, but not muscular. Her short cotton sweater was a shade darker than her blue eyes, and it complemented her fair, flawless complexion. Unlike most women, Hannah wore no jewelry. Not even earrings, he noted as her hair fluttered back when she passed beneath one of the ceiling fans. She didn't need jewels. Not with the way her eyes sparkled.

He felt his eyebrows pull together as he tried to understand why he felt such an overwhelming attraction to this woman. It wasn't as if he hadn't seen a pretty face in five years. So why did his body go to full alert whenever she was around? *What have I gotten myself into? Didn't I learn my lesson when Carmen died?* He had to get a grip on himself, keep everything on a professional level and get out of Charleston as soon as possible, before he did something stupid—again.

When she reached the table, he stood and tossed his napkin on the table. "I'm parked in the alley," he said.

Though his tone was professional, he couldn't seem to keep himself from touching her. He told himself that the only reason he had placed his hand at the small of her back was to lead her toward the rear exit. It had nothing to do with his insatiable need to feel the faint valley of her spine. Or that it brought them close enough so that he could breathe in her floral scent. He told himself he was just being polite. He told himself he was being anything but polite when his body reacted in a predictable and rather embarrassing fashion.

"I've got to be at Joanna's by three," she said as he steered the car onto East Bay. "Tammy made an appointment for me."

He gave her a quick glance. "Why do you look like she arranged your execution? Aren't appointments what lawyers do?"

"Not this lawyer. I normally sit in front of a computer terminal or wade through the law library doing research. I rarely meet clients."

"Sounds boring."

"It's safe," she told him. "I'm the world's worst litigator."

He laughed. "I find it hard to believe that someone as...outspoken as you would have trouble in a courtroom."

"I'm a lousy liar."

"What?" He tried to keep his eyes on the road, but when she shifted in the seat and her skirt hiked up an inch or so, he just couldn't help himself.

"So maybe liar is a bit strong. Let's just say I'm not very good at arguing a cause I don't believe in."

"And they let you graduate from law school with that attitude?"

Her soft laughter filled the car. "I believe in the Constitution, and I'm a good researcher. I knew Rose Porter's home and business addresses less than a day after I found the things in my mother's closet."

Ian checked the mirrors as he made a sudden turn. His action was so abrupt, only the seat belt kept Hannah from tumbling into his lap. "Sorry," he muttered as he again checked the mirrors. When he looked at Hannah, he read the telltale signs of fear around her slightly parted lips and wide eyes. "Don't worry. It looks like your admirer is on his lunch break, because we aren't being tailed."

"Don't even think that," Hannah whispered. "You don't really believe I'm dealing with some sort of stalker, do you?"

Ian shook his head. "Nope. I don't believe in coincidence." He heard her let out a relieved breath. "Which is why I was so curious when I heard you tell Rose about your trips to Charleston as a child. How old were you when they stopped?"

"Five maybe," she answered. "Do you think that's significant?"

"Possibly. It's hard to believe that your parents just happened to take you on vacation back to the place you were born."

"Charleston is a fairly popular vacation spot."

"Then why was it only popular until you were five?" he asked. "What kind of records did your parents keep?"

"There are a lot of boxes I put in storage. They were filled with tax returns, receipts, warranties, stuff like that."

Ian pulled into a public garage across from the Oyster Point Society's grand building. "Can you get someone to send them to you?"

"Why?" she asked once they were out of the car. "I've already told you that my parents weren't well-off."

Ian stopped and looked down at her upturned face. "I'm assuming your father was gainfully employed?"

She nodded. "He was a CPA and my mother was a music teacher in the public school system."

Ian nodded, then asked, "So how come two hardworking people with only one adult child died with enough debt to force the sale of the house?"

Hannah seemed stunned by his question. "What are you getting at?"

He was about to answer, when his eyes caught the small red light of a laser sight passing across Hannah's forehead. His reaction was a fraction faster than the sound of the shot.

Chapter Ten

Her breath left her body in a rush as he knocked her to the ground and fell on top of her. She heard the sound of glass shattering, then another shot rang out. Pieces of concrete pelted her cheek as the second bullet entered the pavement right next to them.

With strength she didn't know she had, Hannah shoved at Ian. She rolled them both to relative safety between two parked cars, just as a third shot hit the exact spot where they had fallen. Then everything went quiet except for the pounding of her heart and Ian's labored breathing.

The silence didn't last long. The garage attendant was screaming and a few people from the street panicked and started yelling. Ian jerked her to a sitting position and seemed to be searching for some injury.

"I'm not hurt," she said when her throat was no longer paralyzed with fear. "What about you?"

He shook his head. What she guessed was concern etched deep lines around his mouth and eyes.

"Obviously, I blew it when I said we hadn't been followed."

The next two hours were a blur of police cars, statements, waiting and being the focal point of passersby. Hannah was grateful when Detective Ross finally appeared and took charge of the situation.

To say Ian had been distant during all the questioning was something of an understatement. He had barely looked at Hannah and, when he did, it was always accompanied by an apologetic bow of his head.

"I can get the two of you out of here," Detective Ross offered.

"Please," Hannah pleaded. "I've got to change and get to Joanna's."

"For what?"

"Her secretary set up an appointment for me," Hannah explained as the detective put her in the passenger seat of his car. Ian sat behind her and remained silent the entire way back to the condo.

Both the detective and Ian went with her into the condo. She could hear them speaking in hushed tones as she tried calling Joanna's office to reschedule the appointment, but only got a recording. Then she remembered that Tammy only worked mornings. Hannah hurriedly changed clothes and brushed dirt, dust and glass shards from her hair. She wasn't exactly in the mood to practice law, but she didn't want to jeopardize Joanna's business. Not when everyone associated with the Rose Tattoo had been so generous to her.

When she appeared in the living room, she was

surprised to find Detective Ross alone. It must have registered on her face, because he quickly said, "Ian went back for his car. I told him I'd see that you got to Joanna's safely."

"Great," she said as she forced a smile to her lips. "But we've got to hurry," she added as she glanced at the clock above the fireplace.

The detective smiled. "One of the perks of the job is using the lights and sirens to aid damsels in distress."

"Distressed is a little mild," she admitted as they left the condo. "The past twenty-four hours have been like a bad dream. Until I came to Charleston, the most dangerous situation I had ever faced was crossing Lake Pontchartrain in a blinding thunderstorm."

"Well, you can't say that now."

His easy manner was like a tonic on her frazzled nerves. By the time they reached Joanna's, Hannah was feeling far less stressed.

The detective followed her to the door, then inside the office. What she thought was a polite gesture suddenly took on a new meaning when she watched him unsnap the holster of his gun and make a sweep of the reception area, the office and then the entire second floor.

"It's just you and me until Ian gets here," the detective said as he sat on the sofa and grabbed a magazine from the coffee table.

Uttering words of thanks, Hannah went into the office and found a neatly typed note from Tammy, along with a file folder, a legal pad and a pen. There was a second stack of motions and other documents that Joanna had left for Hannah to work on, as well as a note requesting she write an appeal on a juvenile case.

Sitting in the rather worn chair, she looked at the framed photograph of Joanna and Gabe that occupied one corner of the desk. They looked happy and serene. "A lot like I used to be," she grumbled at the same time she heard the reception door open.

She knew Joanna had a general practice, but she also knew she did a fair share of criminal-defense work. Judging by the looks of the man coming toward her, Hannah was hoping she remembered enough of the preliminaries of criminal law to do whatever was necessary.

She put him somewhere in his late fifties. She put his clothing somewhere in the late seventies. His polyester shirt was open at the throat, exposing a minimum of seven gold chains and few gray chest hairs. If he had a belt, it was hidden beneath a belly that protruded out like a woman somewhere in her third trimester. His pants were navy and had several white smudges, which was in keeping with the unlit stub of a cigar that dangled from one corner of his mouth.

His cologne arrived a minute before he did. It was almost as unpleasant as the partially smoked cigar smell that filled the air when she rose to greet him.

He shifted a folder and his jacket in order to shake her hand as he smiled. "Billy Pringle, but my friends call me Skeeter."

Hannah winced as his tiger's head pinkie ring

with faux rubies dug into her flesh. "Please have a seat," she said as she closed the door. She didn't miss Detective Ross's rolling eyes as he exaggeratedly waved his hand to clear the air in the wake of the vapor trail left by Skeeter's cologne.

Maybe he was being charged with air pollution, she thought as she returned to her seat. "What can I do for you, Mr. Pringle?"

"Skeeter," he insisted with enthusiasm as he produced a business card. "Pringle Motorcars," he announced, then his smile seemed to fade a bit when she didn't respond to his statement. "Seven stores in and around Charleston. When you buy a car from Pringle, you'll still have cash left over to jingle."

Hannah had the good sense not to groan aloud. "I believe I saw one of your television ads," she said without adding that it had been at three in the morning, and it was so poorly produced that it looked like a tacky home movie.

"Yes, ma'am, largest volume dealerships in the South."

"Fascinating. How can I help you?"

Skeeter gave her a smile that consisted of a display of capped teeth stained yellow by his cigar habit. "I need to get my affairs in order."

"Affairs?"

"I'm game if you are," he said, then gave a hearty belly laugh. When he saw that the comment wasn't appreciated, he tried to cover by switching the laugh into a coughing fit. "I need something to make sure my money goes to my kids and not to any of my ex-wives."

Hannah began to take notes. "How many children do you have?"

"Three...that I know about," he added with a wink.

"And you're divorced?"

"Four and a half times," he joked.

"Half?"

"Got a few more papers to sign," he explained. "She'll be history in another week or so."

Hannah explained her lack of standing in South Carolina, but that didn't seem to discourage the man in the least. "I've brought some of my stuff here," he said as he laid the folder on the desk. "I'll have to get back to you with a complete list of my holdings." With some effort, he hoisted his rotund body out of the chair. Given his weight, and at least one other bad habit she knew of, Hannah wondered if he would live long enough to get back to her.

"You take a gander through this stuff and call to let me know what else you need to do it up right."

Hannah opened the envelope and was almost speechless when she saw the figure listed as his gross income for the previous year. "Of course," she stammered as she reread the seven figures. "I'll be in contact as soon as I have a sense of what would be the best way to minimize probate taxes."

"Sure you will, honey," he said, gripping her

hand again. "And if you're in the market for a new car, you call on Skeeter, you hear?"

Hannah nodded as she followed him to the door. "It was nice to meet you," she said.

"I always like meeting a pretty girl," he said, then cackled his way out the reception door.

Ian scared her when he stepped from the shadow of the doorway. "Was that guy for real? And what the hell is that smell?"

"Eau de Skeeter," Hannah answered. "And don't let his appearance fool you. That guy is worth a fortune. What are you doing here? And where is Detective Ross?"

"Dalton left when I got here. So what did that guy want?"

She eyed him with confusion. "That's privileged. Care to explain why you're talking to me again?"

"When wasn't I talking to you?"

Hannah grunted. "After the shooting. Care to explain why I got the cold shoulder? It wasn't like I was the one firing, you know."

Ian brushed her comment off and held up a scrap of paper with some writing on it. "Guess who I found?"

Hannah went still. "My mother?"

His smile ebbed. "No. But I did find the doctor who signed your phony birth certificate."

"Dr. Longfellow? Really?" she fairly screamed with excitement. Without thinking, Hannah raced to him and threw her arms around his neck. When she attempted to kiss him, she was gently but firmly pushed away. "Sorry," she mumbled. "I guess I forgot myself for a minute."

She had half turned when Ian reached out and took hold of her arm. "Hannah?"

He whispered her name as if it was an apology and that only intensified her humiliation. Using the same gentle firmness, she pulled her arm free. "Let's not do this," she suggested. "I understand."

"Do you?"

Needing to regain a portion of her dignity, she turned, met his eyes and said, "Yes. I understand that your wife died five years ago and I don't compete with ghosts."

He flinched as her words hit him. "It's more complicated than that."

She shook her head. "It doesn't matter, Ian. At least not to me. If you want to martyr yourself to a memory, that's your business. As I said before, as soon as this is over, you'll go back to your hiding place in Montana, and I'll go back to my life in New Orleans. That's the difference between us, Ian." She stepped forward so that she was directly in his face. "You've chosen to use your past as an excuse to hide from the world. To merely exist without feeling, without connections. I've—"

She wanted to believe that the only reason he had grabbed her and brought his mouth down on hers was to shut her up. And maybe that *had* been the reason—at first. However, the instant she felt his warm mouth on hers, it wasn't about anything other than her own suppressed need. His fingers entwined in her hair, forcing her head back even farther. His tongue teased the seam of her lips as he gently moved his palms to her cheeks, cherishing the silky softness of her skin.

His lips moved to brush against the sensitive skin just below her earlobe. The feel of his featherlight kisses drew her stomach into a knot of anticipation. Closing her eyes, Hannah concentrated on the glorious sensations. His grip tightened as his tongue traced a path up to her ear. Her breath caught when he teasingly nibbled the edge of her lobe.

His hands seemed to be everywhere at once until they rested against her rib cage. She swallowed the moan rumbling in her throat. She was aware of everything—his fingers, the feel of his solid body molded against hers, the magical kisses.

"You smell wonderful," he said against her heated skin.

"Ian," she whispered. "I don't think this is such a good idea."

His mouth stilled and he gripped her waist, still holding her in his arms. His eyes were thickly lashed and hooded. A lock of his jet black hair had fallen forward and rested just above his brows. His chiseled mouth was curved in an effortlessly sexy half smile.

"I've kept my hands off you for a reason," he said. He applied pressure to the middle of her back, urging her closer to him again.

"I know," she managed to say above her rapid heartbeat.

"I've tried to pretend I didn't want this. That

last night was just a fluke,'' he continued, punctuating his remark with a kiss on her forehead. ''I look at you and I can't think of anything but this.''

His palms slid up her back until he cradled her face in his hands. Using his thumbs, Ian tilted her head back and hesitated only fractionally before his mouth found hers once more. Instinctively, Hannah's hands went to his waist. She could feel the tapered muscles stiffen in response to her touch.

The scent of soap and cologne filled her nostrils as the exquisite pressure of his mouth increased. His fingers began to slowly massage their way toward her spine. When the tips began a slow, sensual counting of each vertebra, her mind was no longer capable of rational thought. All her attention was homed on the intense sensations filling her with fierce desire.

With her heart racing in her ears, she allowed herself to revel in the feel of his strong body against hers. As he deepened the kiss into something more demanding, she succumbed to the potent dose of longing.

She began to explore the solid contours of his body beneath his soft cotton shirt. It was like feeling the smooth, sculpted surface of a granite statue. Everywhere she touched she felt the distinct outline of corded muscle. She could even feel the vibration from his erratic pulse.

All her wondering if he, too, felt the strong tug of attraction was easily erased by the undeniable proof of his arousal pressing against her belly.

Her heart soared with the knowledge that Ian so obviously felt aroused, too.

When he lifted his hand, she had to fight to keep from giving in to her strong urge to pull him back to her. His eyes met and held hers as he quietly looked down, searching her face. His breaths were coming in short, almost raspy gulps and she watched the tiny vein at his temple race in time with her own rapid heartbeat.

"I didn't want to do this," he said.

Hannah's eyes flew open wider and her expression must have registered obvious hurt.

Ian's chuckle was deep and reached his eyes.

"I meant I didn't want to do this because I knew it wouldn't be enough," he corrected. "I've been able to control myself for years, but being around you has changed that. I'm supposed to be doing a job for a friend."

"And you think a few kisses will affect your ability to do what you promised Gabe?"

"I hope not," he said as he claimed her mouth again. His kiss lasted for several heavenly moments. "I just don't know if kissing you will be enough."

"I don't think we have to worry about that right now. This is all so sudden and new, and maybe it's nothing more than chemistry," she suggested as she rested her cheek against his chest.

"I can ignore chemistry, Hannah, but I don't seem to be able to ignore *you*."

"Thank you, I think," she said against the soft fabric covering his broad chest. "Why don't you try not to analyze it, Ian. We're both responsible, consenting adults. All we did was kiss."

"All we did was kiss?" he countered as his thumb hooked under her chin. "It seems like a lot more than that to me, and I've got to tell you, it scares the hell out of me."

She tried to ignore the sudden tightness in the pit of her stomach. "Seems or feels?" she challenged as she stepped out of his embrace.

TWO DAYS LATER they were on their way to a planned community just north of Hilton Head Island. For Ian it had been a frustrating two days in every conceivable sense of the word. Hannah's accusations had hit a little too close to the mark.

"I think they were a group of colossal snobs, who ought to be sued for their sexist attitudes," she fumed as she sat next to him.

He glanced over and smiled. She was like a little ball of fire with her arms crossed and her brow all furrowed. "It's a private men's club," he reminded her. "You're the attorney—you ought to know that if they aren't federally funded, they can exclude whomever they want."

"But they wouldn't even let me in the foyer!" Hannah cried. "Do you know how insulting it was to stand on the street while you—by virtue of your sex alone—were granted entrance?"

He patted her knee. "I told you already, all I got was the ten-cent tour. Apparently, the Oyster Point Society isn't taking any new members."

"What exactly is the Oyster Point Society?" she asked.

Ian sighed and said, "The guy I spoke to said he was just the caretaker and all he added was they do philanthropic deeds for native Charlestonians."

"They need a two-story Georgian mansion that takes up nearly an entire city block to be philanthropic?" He smelled her shampoo as she angrily tossed her hair back. "What did he say when you showed him the lapel pin?"

"He showed me the door," Ian told her. "He did try to get me to leave the pin, though. Apparently, they don't care for nonmembers having one."

"Too bad they don't have a female caretaker, you could have charmed your way in and gotten a look around."

"Stop grousing," he said. "I got enough of a look around to know that there are fire stairs that lead to the second floor."

"I hope you aren't suggesting that we break and enter? I am an officer of the court, Ian. I could get disbarred for committing a felony."

"Can you think of another option?"

"I will," she promised him. "Didn't they train you to gain access to private areas when you were with the CIA?"

He smiled at her. "Yeah, I learned how to break and enter."

"Wonderful. I can't tell you what that does to my opinion of our government."

"How about giving me an opinion regarding the map?" he suggested. "I don't want to miss the turn."

Hannah directed him through the planned community with streets named after some of the greatest golfers in history, or so Ian informed her. Of course, Hannah recognized only those more recent celebrities, as in Arnold Palmer Court, where Dr. Longfellow lived.

They parked in front of a single-story home with a professionally landscaped yard that matched the other single-story homes with professionally landscaped yards on the dead-end street. Hannah reached the door first and rang the bell.

A small woman dressed in uniform answered. She greeted them in heavily accented English. Hannah was about to ask for the doctor, when Ian began a dialogue with the woman in rapid-fire Spanish.

Thanks to her high-school foreign-language requirement, she understood just enough to know that the doctor wasn't in. She also understood the definition of flirting when Ian gave the young woman's hand a kiss, then the two carried on a hushed exchange.

"That was pretty sleazy," she whispered as she got into the car.

"What?" he asked with feigned innocence.

"I know I commented on your failure to utilize your charm, but don't you think you went a little overboard with that poor girl?"

He chuckled. "Okay, as penance for inappropriate behavior, I won't tell you where Dr. Longfellow is."

"I take it back," she chimed happily. "Where is he?"

"Playing in a tournament at the club."

Hannah reached out and touched his hand where it rested on the console. "How far were you willing to go to get that information out of her?"

He pretended to be insulted. "A gentleman never tells, remember?"

"Uh-huh," she murmured as she glanced down at the map to get her bearings. "The club is up to the left. How will we find the good doctor?" Hannah asked as they pulled into the parking lot. "Don't all golfers dress alike?"

Ian laughed. "The direct approach is probably the best."

"The direct approach?" she asked as they got out of the car.

He winked at her. "Yeah, we'll go in and ask for him."

The Oaks Country Club was a huge building with a main floor housing a pro shop, gift shop and a modest restaurant. According to the young man who escorted them, the top floor was a ballroom reserved for functions like private parties or the monthly social. The lower floor was where the dressing rooms, showers, saunas and cart return were, and the young man said he would check there to see where Dr. Longfellow and his foursome were.

Ian ordered a beer, while she asked for water as she gazed out over the lovely setting. There were palm trees and small lagoons, and everything was brilliantly green except for the sand traps that dotted the course. "It almost makes you want to take up the game," she murmured.

"Not me," he said. "It takes too long."

She regarded Ian for a long time before asking, "What do you do to pass the time?"

"I can tell you've never been to a working cattle ranch."

"I don't even like ranch salad dressing."

Ignoring the frosted mug, he took a long swallow from the bottle, which, judging by the reaction of the few patrons in the bar, just wasn't done in this upper-crust playground. "It's a lot of work. Most of it physical."

"And dirty and smelly, I'll bet."

His smile was breathtaking. "That, too."

"How long did you work for the CIA?"

The smile faded. "I went to the FBI academy and they recruited me there. I was twenty-three, and those were the days when we believed the war against drugs was more than just a handy campaign slogan."

"You sound quite jaded."

He shrugged and traced his thumbnail around the condensation that had formed on his beer bottle. "Realistic. At least in terms of what really went on. We knew who was producing, importing and selling most of the junk, but that Constitution you are so fond of makes it impossible for us to touch most of the high-level guys."

"I didn't write it," Hannah defended. "Maybe you should have worked harder to get the laws changed."

He gave her a hard stare. "Most politicians are quick to say they want to make appropriate law, but the ACLU and/or the Supreme Court always manages to step in."

Hannah looked up and, suddenly, any notion of defending the system, flawed though it might be, went right out of her head. "You remember what you said about not believing in coincidence?" she asked.

"Yeah, and?"

"Turn around."

Chapter Eleven

"Well, I was right!" Skeeter Pringle said as he gave a hearty slap on the back to the young man who had escorted them into the bar.

Skeeter was with a very distinguished man in dark tinted glasses, whom Hannah guessed was the doctor. "How...unexpected to see you here," she said as she rose. "Ian MacPhearson, this is Skeeter Pringle, the client you might have seen leaving the other day."

That comment drew a strange reaction from Skeeter's companion, but he appeared to recover quickly. While Skeeter was busy giving Ian a sales pitch for a car, Hannah extended her hand to the other gentleman and said, "I'm Hannah Bailey. It's nice to meet you, Dr. Longfellow."

He took her hand, but she couldn't tell if his smile made it all the way to his shrouded eyes. "I'm afraid there has been some sort of misunderstanding, Miss...Bailey, was it?"

"Hannah," she returned politely.

The young attendant spoke up then. "Mr. Pringle and his foursome were just coming in, and when they heard me mention your name, Mr. Pringle said you were friends. Dr. Longfellow is on sixteen. He should be through in about a half an hour.'' The young man dashed away quickly, sort of like a young, male version of Joleen and her hasty exits.

''Bring us the usual!'' Skeeter called to the bartender. ''And another cold one for my new friend here.''

''I'm Jeffrey Fielding,'' the man said as they moved to a table large enough to accommodate them all. ''What sort of legal work are you doing, Miss Bailey? Funny—'' he paused and stroked his perfectly clean-shaven face ''—I don't recall seeing your name in my bar files.''

''Jeff here is an attorney, too,'' Skeeter announced with a hearty slap on the thinner man's back. ''Only he's about to be appointed a judge, so I guess that means I won't have to worry about those speeding tickets, eh, Jeff ol' boy?''

''I'm really not doing the legal work,'' Hannah answered. ''I'm from out of state, and I'm really just handling the preliminary paperwork as a favor to a friend. I work in New Orleans.'' When she named her firm, it did get a small reaction out of Fielding, though he quickly returned to his stony mask.

''Who is the friend you're assisting? Perhaps I know him,'' Fielding asked as the bartender delivered highball glasses to Skeeter and Fielding, as well as another beer to the uncharacteristically quiet Ian.

"Her. Joanna Boudreaux. Or maybe Langston, I'm not sure if she uses her married name."

Upon hearing the name, Fielding looked as if he'd just smelled an unpleasant odor. "Boudreaux, I believe, is her preference. She has a reputation for taking on whoever will pay for her services."

"That must be why Mr. Pringle sought her out instead of you," Hannah said with a bright smile. It wasn't as if she knew Joanna all that well, it was that she knew men like Fielding well enough to feel the need to defend a sister attorney.

"My practice is corporate work mostly. Though I've been slowly easing my clients to my partners or other qualified practitioners since my nomination to the bench."

And Hannah would have bet her last dime that not one of those clients was referred to a woman. Fielding was one of those overtly sexist types who gave all men a bad name. His smug, superior attitude, coupled with his overpriced golfing outfit in a brilliant chartreuse, made her dislike him immediately. Skeeter was gross, but at least he didn't put on airs.

Lord, I can't believe I'm actually comparing someone to Skeeter Pringle, and Skeeter wins! "I didn't expect to see you again so soon," Hannah said to her pseudo-client.

"Play this tournament every year, don't we, Jeff?"

His friend nodded as he drained the highball glass and showed it to the bartender as a silent request for a refill.

"The proceeds benefit some of them...what do you call them now? Mentally challenged people," Skeeter announced. "If I'd have known you were headed this way, you coulda hitched a ride with me." Skeeter glanced at Ian and added, "Your friend, too, 'course."

"'Course," Ian agreed. "Then I guess you gentlemen know Dr. Longfellow?"

"It's long past time for ol' doc to hang up his irons," Skeeter said with a hearty laugh. "He's got to be pushing eighty, and he's lucky if he only shoots twice his age."

Skeeter laughed, Fielding remained rigid, Ian smiled and Hannah didn't have a clue about the joke until Ian leaned close to her ear and whispered, "The point of the game is to have the lowest score."

She smiled as she tried not to let the tingling sensation where his breath had warmed her ear distract her.

"We have to go turn in our cards," Fielding said with a pointed look at Skeeter. "Nice to have met you, Miss Bailey, sir."

Skeeter left reluctantly, and Fielding took his drink with him. "That was a little weird," Hannah said.

Ian checked his watch and said, "The doctor will still be a few minutes. I want to go check something out."

"But..."

He was already out the door before she could argue. She spent the next ten minutes smiling at the various groups who sauntered into the bar.

She got to listen to snippets of conversations about birdies and bogies and a bunch of other golfing terms that were like a foreign language.

Ian returned wearing a satisfied grin.

"What gives?" she asked.

Ian was about to tell her, when the young attendant returned, escorting a rather frail-looking man. Hannah politely listened to the introductions, then invited the elderly gentleman to join them.

"It isn't every day I have a pretty lady waiting for me when I come off the course," he said with genuine courtesy. "To what do I owe this honor?"

They waited until the doctor had ordered a gin and tonic before Hannah reached into her purse and slid the birth certificate across the table.

The doctor checked three places before he found his glasses. When he slipped them on, his watered-down blue eyes appeared to be the size of half-dollars. She wondered how the man could play a game like golf if his vision was so poor.

He read the certificate, then smiled at her. "It appears this is not the first time we've met then."

"I was hoping you could tell me something about my delivery."

Dr. Longfellow looked at her as if she had asked him to explain quantum physics. "This is more than thirty-one years ago! Do you know how many babies I delivered in fifty-three years in practice?"

"No," she answered.

"Neither do I." The doctor sighed as he removed his glasses. "Why did you come to me?"

Hannah explained about her parents' deaths and discovering that she had been adopted. "I've met the woman whose name is listed on there, but I have concrete proof that she wasn't the woman who gave birth to me."

The doctor reached out and patted her hand with his arthritis-gnarled fingers. "I was head of obstetrics then. I signed a lot of birth certificates. I also delivered a lot of babies for girls who had gotten into trouble." He paused and lowered his voice. "It wasn't like it is now," he said. "Having a baby out of wedlock was nothing to be proud of. In those days, the girl's family said she went off to visit an aunt. The baby was usually placed with a good home."

"Do you remember which homes?" Hannah asked.

"Half of the time I didn't know whether the girls were keeping their babies or not. Unless they told me, I didn't ask. Most of the time I was occupied with the delivery."

"What about the Charleston Girls' Home?" she pressed.

"Sure," the doctor said. "We provided free services to them. It looked good for the hospital and the director was Society, so we—"

"Oyster Point Society?" Ian interrupted.

The doctor nodded. "Back then, we were a pretty tight-knit group. It isn't like that anymore, though. Now it's a bunch of yuppies sharing stock tips. I almost never go up for the monthly luncheons anymore."

Hannah was about to mention her lapel pin, when she felt Ian's hand on her leg beneath the table. He gave her a small, warning squeeze, then casually said, "Is that how you know Skeeter Pringle and Jeffrey Fielding?"

The doctor made a derisive sound. "There was a third one. If you ask me, they should have tossed them all when they tossed Skeeter."

"Skeeter is a little rough around the edges," Ian continued. "He told me it wasn't his fault."

"That wouldn't surprise me," the doctor agreed. "Pringle, Fielding and that other one were trouble from the word *go*." The doctor paused again. "But they all seem to have settled down."

"But you don't remember the third man?" Hannah asked.

The doctor took a final swallow of his drink and struggled to a standing position. "Sorry. But ask Jeffrey. They usually play together. I was pretty surprised when he teamed up with Skeeter. You'd think a man with his eye on the governor's seat would steer clear of a man who got tossed from his own club on charges of violating our moral code. Only time it's ever happened," he added as an attendant appeared at his side. "Sorry I couldn't help you more, young lady."

Ian was staring at her after the doctor had gone.

"Is something wrong? I can't believe I'm about to say this, but what if it turns out that Skeeter Pringle is my father?" She actually shivered.

Ian tossed a few dollars on the table and said,

"I guess that would make you an automobile dealership heiress."

"That isn't funny."

Ian chuckled. "Actually, it is. Maybe Skeeter will make you his spokesmodel."

"Maybe I'll kill you, if you don't shut up."

"IAN SAID YOU WERE supposed to stay here," Rose argued as Hannah collected her purse and the keys to her replacement rental.

"The man is a client." *And if there is a God, he isn't my father.* "He has the rest of the documents I need to work up an estate plan. Skeeter Pringle could be a big client for Joanna. I don't want to—"

Rose's green eyes grew wide. "Not Skeeter Pringle from the TV?"

"Yes," She sighed. "One and the same."

"I wouldn't buy a dog from that man," Rose said. "Is he as nasty and sweaty as he looks on the television?"

"Unfortunately."

"Joanna's probably seen those tacky ads he does. I don't think she'd care if you alienated a pig like him."

"He's a pretty rich pig," Hannah explained. "At least, he is on paper," she muttered.

"Have him meet you here," Rose pleaded. "You can use my office."

"Thanks," Hannah said as she gave Rose a warm smile. "But I've already been around Skeeter, so I think we can cross him off the list of suspects." *Unless we're talking about paternity.*

"I'm paging Ian," Rose threatened.

"Be my guest. Tell him I'll see him back at the condo later. This shouldn't take more than a few minutes. It's been two days since anyone followed me. Maybe whoever it was got tired and gave up."

A short while later, Hannah pulled her compact into the driveway just as dusk painted the sky a pretty shade of pink. The flowers along the walkway entertained her with their fragrance as she fumbled with the keys to the office. When she heard a car slowing behind her, she turned and immediately recognized the Pringle Motorcars plate on the front of the big, blue Cadillac. She let out her breath, furious that she still felt such fear when she had every reason to believe that the brazen shooting at the parking garage had somehow dissuaded whoever had been following her.

"Evening, Hannah," Skeeter greeted as he joined her on the front stoop. "Thanks for meeting me after hours. Your young man didn't mind? Or is he meeting you here? I don't believe I've ever seen you without that strapping guy somewhere close by."

"Ian is off doing something," she answered evasively. "Let's get started," she suggested as she opened the door and entered, with Skeeter following closely on her heels.

Hannah was already standing behind the desk when her brain began to process the situation. By the time she realized that Skeeter had set up the meeting to deliver papers and had nothing in his hands, it was too late. His eyes were bulging, his face red with fury, as he lunged for her, hands outstretched and aiming for her throat.

Chapter Twelve

She was watching his eyes as his hands gripped her throat. He looked like something out of a horror film with his rasping breath and fiendish stare.

Then his eyes seemed to gloss over, he went ghostly white and, before she had even recovered enough to fight him off, he lay at her feet in a heap.

That was how Ian found them.

"Your neck!" he thundered as he raced to the motionless form of Skeeter and roughly turned him faceup.

"I didn't touch him," Hannah exclaimed. Her hands went to her throat as she heard the gravelly sound of her own voice. "He was attacking me and he...he...just fell down!"

"Call an ambulance," Ian instructed. "And the cops."

When she didn't move, Ian abandoned Skeeter and dialed the emergency number himself.

For the third time in a week, Hannah was faced with explaining to Detective Ross a set of bizarre events that usually only happened in soap operas.

At first, she and Ian had been separated, then, once the paramedics determined that Skeeter had suffered a stroke, they were reunited.

Hannah sat on the sofa, feeling safe in the cradle of Ian's large body.

"We'll have to take some pictures of your neck," Detective Ross said. "If he recovers, we'll need them as evidence."

"My neck?" Hannah repeated in a daze.

Ian traced his finger gently around her throat. "You're pretty bruised. Let them take the pictures," he said with a faint smile. "We wouldn't want some shyster lawyer getting him off for lack of evidence, now, would we?"

For the first time in hours, Hannah laughed. A female evidence technician escorted her upstairs and then shot the bruises from every conceivable angle. She was appreciative of the deference and thanked the detective before she and Ian left for the condo.

"I guess I don't have to wonder who's been after me anymore," she said as they drove toward what she was beginning to think of as home. "I also guess this means Skeeter is probably my father. Why else would he attack me?"

"I think it would be a good idea if you didn't think too much for the rest of the night."

She glanced at the silhouette of his handsome profile. "Meaning?"

"What you need is a hot bath and a decent night's sleep. We can sort Skeeter and his motives out in the morning."

"I suppose," she murmured as they reached the condo and took the elevator to the penthouse.

"Do you want the pool first?" she asked, hoping it sounded like a joke and not an invitation. For some reason, she didn't want to be apart from him. It was probably just the trauma, but still, even once he had said no, she wanted to move, but her feet refused to cooperate.

"Go on," he urged.

"Okay." Hannah reluctantly went to her room, took the things she needed for a shower and realized her hand still had a slight tremor. She sensed him behind her and turned slowly.

Ian stood in the doorway, looking as uncertain as she felt. He didn't enter the room, but he didn't leave, either.

"Should I hurry?" Hannah asked when she could no longer stand the silence.

He moved toward her and said, "No need. We have all the time in the world."

Did he have to speak in that low, seductive tone? Her throat went suddenly dry—a stark contrast to the clamminess of her palms. Every muscle in her body seemed to tense with an awareness of the man just a few feet away. She stood frozen, teetering on the brink of indecision. She seemed to melt like soft butter whenever he so much as looked in her direction. It was incredible. Hannah didn't have casual affairs. She couldn't even recall the last time she had even been on a date. For some reason that was completely foreign to her, Ian had only to look at her with those sexy eyes and she was more than ready to throw herself into his arms. *When did I become the desperate old maid my mother always claimed I'd be?*

Hannah tossed her items onto the floor without care. Balling her hands into fists at her side, she shifted her weight from foot to foot, then said, "This won't work."

"What?"

"I don't have the nerve to ask you, and you don't seem to have the nerve to ask me, and I'm getting tired of pretending I'm immune where you're concerned."

Ian didn't respond immediately. He simply leaned against the wall as if he didn't have a care in the world. "Ask me what?"

Her eyes roamed boldly over the vast expanse of his shoulders, drinking in the sight of his shirt where it was pulled tightly across the contours of his impressive upper body. She openly admired the powerful thighs straining against the soft fabric of his jeans. The mere sight caused a fluttering in the pit of her stomach. "To... The two of us have this...this...*this* between us." She took two breaths to calm her rapid pulse. "My self-control seems to go right out the window whenever you're around. I hate laying here every night knowing you're in the next room. Knowing that I'd rather have you in my room."

"All you had to do was ask, Hannah," he said with silky softness. "I've wanted you from the first moment I saw you."

Her bravado was slipping. "But we aren't children," she insisted. "We can't have everything we want. Maybe we should think about this some more."

"Does that mean you don't want me?"

Hannah closed her eyes briefly. "It means I'm very confused. It means I'm scared about the way you make me feel. It means I know better than to get involved with someone with your kind of baggage. It means I don't sleep around, and I don't know why I can't seem to stop thinking about being with you when I know that you'll probably be on a plane back to Montana soon."

"Forget all that other stuff, Hannah. It doesn't matter, at least not tonight."

She was helpless when he spoke to her like that. When he was kind and gentle, he was too perfect for words. She looked up at him. Summoning the last remnants of her self-control, she said, "I think it would be best if we went to our own rooms right now."

"Best for whom?"

"For both of us."

"Not from my standpoint, Hannah. I've been thinking about what it would be like to spend the night with you in my arms."

She glared at him, but softened it with a smile. "You aren't making this any easier."

"I'm sorry," he said as he moved and pulled her into his arms. "But I'm not going to lie to you. I haven't been able to think of much of anything but you for days."

Protected in the circle of his arms, Hannah closed her eyes and allowed her cheek to rest against his chest. Would it be so awful to take what he was so willing to give? She could forget about the awful scene with Skeeter. Forget everything but the way he made her feel. She could keep this memory in her heart always. This might be her only chance.

His fingers danced over the outline of her spine, leaving a trail of electrifying sensation in their wake. Like a spring flower, passion flourished and blossomed from deep within her, filling her quickly with a type of frenzied desire she had never before known. He ignited feelings so powerful and so intense that Hannah fleetingly wondered if this was love. Then he touched her and she couldn't think anymore.

Ian moved his hand in a series of slow, sensual circles until it rested against her rib cage, just under the swell of her breast. He wanted—no, needed—to see her face. He wanted to see the desire in her eyes. Catching her chin between his thumb and forefinger, he tilted her head up with the intention of searching her eyes. He never made it that far.

His eyes were riveted to her lips, which were slightly parted, a glistening shade of pale pink. His eyes roamed over every delicate feature, and he could feel her heart rate increase through the thin fabric of her blouse. A knot formed in his throat as he silently acknowledged his own incredible need for this woman.

Lowering his head, he was finally able to take that first, tentative taste. Her mouth was warm and pliant; so was her body, which now pressed urgently against him. His hands roamed purposefully, memorizing every nuance and curve.

He felt his own body respond with an ache, then an almost overwhelming rush of desire surged through him. Her arms slid around his waist, pulling him closer. Ian marveled at the perfect way they fit together. It was as if Hannah had been made for this. For him.

"Hannah," he whispered against her mouth. He toyed with a lock of her hair first, then slowly wound his hand through the silken mass and gave a gentle tug, forcing her head back even more. Looking down at her face, Ian knew there was no other sight on earth as beautiful and inviting as her smoky blue eyes.

In one effortless motion, he lifted her and carefully lowered her onto the bed. Her pale, golden hair fanned out against the pillow.

"I think you're supposed to get on the bed with me," Hannah said in a husky voice.

With a single finger, Ian reached out to trace the delicate outline of her mouth. Her skin was the color of ivory, with a faint rosy flush. "Are you sure?" he asked in a tight voice, not sure how he would handle it if she uttered a rejection. He sucked in a breath and waited for her response.

"Very."

"Good." He fumbled with the pocket of his jeans, leaving the foil packet on the nightstand for later.

"Do condoms have a shelf life of five years?" she teased.

"I wouldn't know, since I bought these here,

after I kissed you,'' he said with a wink. Sliding into place next to her, he began showering her face with light kisses. Carefully, he kissed each bruise until his mouth searched and found a sensitive spot at the base of her throat. He felt her fingers working the buttons of his shirt and prayed he could make this last. He wanted to go slowly, linger over every delectable inch of her beautiful body. He wanted to commit her to memory. He wasn't sure why, but it seemed to his passion-soaked brain that this was different. This wasn't just sex.

He waited breathlessly for the feel of her hands on his body, and he wasn't disappointed when the anticipation gave way to reality. A pleasurable moan spilled from his mouth when she brushed away his clothing and began running her palms over the taut muscles of his stomach.

Capturing both of her hands in one of his, Ian gently held them above her head. The position arched her back, drawing his eyes down to the outline of her erect nipples.

''This isn't fair,'' she said as he slowly undid the buttons of her blouse.

''Believe me, Hannah. If I let you keep touching me, I'd probably last less than a minute.'' He reassured her with a smile and a kiss. ''Cut me a break, here. I can't fight you and my raging hormones.''

Hannah responded by giving a sensual little laugh before lifting her body to him. The rounded swell of one partially exposed breast brushed his arm. He began peeling away the remaining layers of her clothing. He was rewarded by the incredible sight of her breasts spilling over the edges of a lacy bra. His eyes burned as he drank in the sight of the taut peaks straining against the lace. His hand rested first against the flatness of her stomach before inching up over the warm flesh. Finally, his fingers closed over the rounded fullness.

"Please let me touch you!" Hannah cried out.

"Not yet," he whispered as his thumb and forefinger released the front clasp on her bra. He ignored her futile struggle to release her hands, as he dipped his head to kiss the raging pulse point at her throat. Her soft skin grew hot as he worked his mouth lower and lower. She gasped when his mouth closed around her nipple, then called his name in a hoarse voice that caused a tremor to run the full length of his body.

Moments later, he lifted his head only long enough to see her wild expression and to tell her she was beautiful.

"So are you."

Whether it was the sound of her voice or possibly the way she pressed herself against him, Ian didn't know or care. He found himself nearly undone by the level of passion communicated by the movements of her supple body.

He reached down until his fingers made contact with a wisp of silk and lace. The feel of the sensuous garment against his skin very nearly pushed him over the edge. With her help, he was able to whisk the panties over her hips and legs, until she was finally next to him without a single barrier.

He sought her mouth again as he released his hold on her hands. He didn't know which was more potent, the feel of her naked body against him, or the frantic way she worked to remove the rest of his clothing. His body moved to cover hers, his tongue thrust deeply into the warm recesses of her mouth. His hand moved downward, skimming the side of her body all the way to her thigh. Then, giving in to the urgent need pulsating through him, Ian positioned himself between her legs. Every muscle in his body tensed as he looked at her face before directing his attention lower to the point where they would join. Hannah lifted her hips, welcoming, inviting, as her palms flattened against his hips and tugged him toward her.

"I wish it could be this way forever." He groaned against her lips.

"Don't think about forever," she whispered back. "Not now. Just make love to me, please?"

He wasted no time responding to her request. After retrieving the foil packet and doing what was necessary, he entered her in a single motion. He thrust deeply inside her, each time knowing without question that he had found heaven on earth.

He wanted to treat her to a slow, building climax, but with the feelings sweeping through him, it wasn't an option. He caught his breath and held it. The sheer pleasure of being inside of her sweet softness was just too powerful. Apparently, he wasn't the only one suffering. She wrapped her legs around his hips and he felt her body convulse just as the first explosive waves surged from him. One after the other, ripples of pleasure poured from him into her. Satisfaction had never been so sweet.

With his head buried next to hers, the sweet scent of her hair filled his nostrils. It was quite a while before Ian reluctantly relinquished possession of her body. It took several more minutes before his breathing slowed to a steady, satiated pace. He started to say something, when Hannah simply placed her finger against his lips and whispered, "It was perfect."

IN THE HAZE between sleep and consciousness, Hannah's mind slowly retrieved a litany of conflicting images. Wrapping herself in the warmth of the comforter, her eyes remained shut as she began to replay the dream in her mind.

There were flashes of Magnolia Gardens mingled with a face. Then flashes of the fulfilling passion she had shared with Ian. Her eyes opened to find sunlight streaming into the room. Her hand slid across the soft sheets, fully expecting to make contact with Ian's warm, hard body. Instead, she found nothing but cool fabric.

Instantly awake, she sat up, brushing the tangled mass of hair out of her face. She was alone.

"At least we don't have to do that awkward morning-after thing," she grumbled as she left the bed for the bathroom.

Her reflection was something of a shock. Gingerly, she touched the faint, purplish handprints clearly visible and pressed to test the sensitivity.

It looked worse than it was, which somehow seemed of little comfort as she slipped into the shower.

As the warm water pulsed over her, Hannah struggled with her dilemma. Ian would no doubt be leaving soon. Since the only logical conclusion for Skeeter's attack was that he was her father, it wouldn't take very long to determine who her biological mother was. Skeeter must have thought she'd come after him for support or something. Hannah raked her fingers through her hair, knowing that final piece of the puzzle that was her life would satisfy whatever debt Ian felt he owed his friend Gabe. She tried to tell herself to be adult about the whole thing. She'd known from the start that her association with Ian was temporary. It wasn't as if she was some teenager mooning after the class hunk. She was too old and too realistic to give those thoughts validity.

Turning her face up into the spray, she hoped she could wash away the feeling of emptiness that came with the knowledge that her time with him was about to end. She could handle it, she told herself. This was the casual fling most of her girlfriends raved about following their vacations. She had to keep it in its proper perspective. Knowing she should be adult about the whole thing was easier said than done. The idea of never seeing those stunning blue-gray eyes or hearing his laugh brought a rush of tears.

The fierceness of the emotion she was feeling had to be some sort of delayed reaction to the events of the past week. She was crying as a form of release. It was probably good for her soul.

Oh, crap! her voice of reason challenged. *I'm crying because I don't want this to end. I don't want Ian out of my life.*

"And the alternative is what?" she whispered as she shampooed her hair. "Beg him to return to New Orleans with me?" That wasn't an option. To even make the suggestion would mean she would have to tell him the truth. Telling the truth would mean admitting to herself that she had fallen in love with him in less time than it takes to have a suit altered. Even if he did feel something for her, she doubted a man who had spent five years chastely grieving could even be capable of giving her the kind of love she wanted. The fairy tale she and every other girl dreamed. *Way to screw up your life, Hannah,* she thought with a healthy dose of self-disgust. *Only you would be stupid enough to fall for a man with emotional scars that probably ran too deep to ever heal.*

Toweling her hair, she frowned at her reflection. "Do I walk out there, face him and act as if it was no big deal? As if last night was just a casual thing?" That would be a little hard to pull off.

She used the dryer on her hair, dressed in black slacks and a white blouse and made the bed. "You're hiding," she told herself. "Be brave and just get it over with." Taking a deep breath, she plastered a smile on her face and followed the aroma of coffee.

Ian was in the kitchen, shirtless and sipping

coffee as he sat reading the newspaper. His hair was mussed and the dark stubble on his chin told her that he hadn't yet shaved. When he turned and looked at her, she realized there was something else he hadn't done—slept.

Rubbing her hands together nervously, she met his stare directly and asked, "Are we going to have one of those uncomfortable moments where neither one of us knows what to say to the other?"

His smile, though strained, did little to relieve her tension. "I've been practicing a little speech half the night. Want to hear it?"

"Not before I have coffee," she responded. Her intuition told her that if it had taken him half the night to prepare, it probably wasn't anything good.

When she stepped into the galleyway of the kitchen, she noticed the stack of open cardboard boxes just inside the front door. "Is that your luggage?" she asked on a nervous little laugh.

His expression was impossible to read. He looked so tired, and yet she got the impression that his thinking wasn't nearly as dull as his bloodshot eyes. "Nope. The return address is from a Cindy Halperin, New Orleans."

"Nawlens," she teased. "I called Cindy for those records I told you about. But I guess my parents' financial history is pretty irrelevant in light of Skeeter's attack."

"How's your throat?"

"I'll be wearing high necklines for a while,"

she answered. "But it doesn't hurt. I want to call the hospital to see how he's doing."

Ian folded the newspaper and tossed it aside. "I already did that. He's on a respirator and it doesn't look good."

"I guess I should feel *something.* I don't think I'll be able to do that until I understand why he'd want to kill his own child."

"Aren't you jumping to conclusions?"

She leaned against the long counter that separated them. "If he isn't my father, why would he want to kill me? You didn't see his face," she recalled with a shudder. "If he hadn't stroked out, he would have strangled me. He was almost crazed looking. Since I'd never met the man, I can't think of another explanation."

Ian rounded the countertop, stood behind her, then folded her against his warm body. His chin rested against the top of her head and she let her eyes flutter closed, enjoying the comfort of his embrace.

"I made a few other calls this morning."

Her heart sank into her feet as she felt a gentle vibration when the words fell from his mouth. Placing her cup on the counter, she traced the outline of his large hands with her fingers. "What time is your flight?"

Ian spun her around, placed his hand beneath her chin and forced her to meet his eyes. "Flight?"

"Back to the ranch?" she prompted. "It shouldn't be too hard for me to find my mother now that I know about Skeeter. I really appreciate your help and—"

The kiss was brief and unexpected. When he lifted his head, Hannah still had her eyes wide-open. Ian's head tilted to one side and a frown creased his brow. "Did you think I was going to race out the door after last night?"

"The thought crossed my mind," she admitted. "It's not like we made a commitment. We had sex."

His sexy, lopsided grin reached his eyes. "We had *great* sex."

It took no time for her face to heat with a blush. "Yes, we did," she said, though she had to break eye contact before she was capable of such an open admission. "I was just trying to reassure you that what happened between us didn't have any strings attached to it."

"Really?" His jovial tone was grating.

"I'm trying very hard to make this as easy on you as possible. I'd think you could show a little decency and just let the subject drop."

He released her. "I will…for now. But only because I've had an opportunity to review those financial records."

Hannah turned back to her coffee. "I'll bet that was fascinating reading."

"The year you were adopted, your parents withdrew over twenty thousand dollars from their savings accounts and their retirement funds."

"They bought me?" she asked as she nearly dropped her coffee cup.

When she next turned to Ian, it was to watch

as he went to the boxes and pulled out a stack of papers and canceled checks. "Come here," he said as he motioned her to the dining room table.

Ian methodically laid out a series of checks and bank statements that covered the time of her birth, straight through to the time of their deaths.

She scanned the numbers, and on a breath of disbelief, she whispered, "No wonder they died broke."

"Look at the dates," Ian said. "Notice anything *coincidental?*"

"They didn't start buying cashier's checks until I was five," Hannah replied. "Which is about the same time they stopped bringing me to Charleston." She looked up at him and asked, "Do you think Skeeter was blackmailing them?"

"Didn't Skeeter give you his tax returns and financial statements that first day?" When she nodded, he suggested, "Then we should go and see if Skeeter made any deposits that coincide with the cashier's checks your parents bought."

Hannah agreed, then said, "I had a dream last night."

Ian gave her a devilish grin. "It wasn't a dream."

Hannah ignored him. "I haven't had *this* dream in years."

"We could probably ask that wacky waitress Susan from the Rose Tattoo. I'll bet she's well versed in dream interpretation."

Hannah shook her head as flashes of the dream played in her mind. "I don't think it's a dream. I think it's a memory."

"Of what?"

"The trips to Magnolia Gardens. There's a man talking to my mother."

"Skeeter?"

"That's the strange part. I don't think so. The man was old. I haven't thought about him in years."

Ian brushed a wayward strand of hair from her face. "If you were only four or five, it could have been Skeeter. Young children generally think of anyone over eighteen as being ancient."

Hannah shook her head again, completely sure now that she had run the memory through her mind a few more times. "It wasn't Skeeter."

"There's one way we can find out for sure." He gently brushed her cheek with the back of his hand. "How do you feel about giving blood?"

"DNA?" she asked. "But that would require a sample from Skeeter, and he isn't in any shape to consent to a paternity test."

"Rose's niece is a doctor at the hospital where Skeeter is a guest."

"That isn't legal," Hannah reminded him.

"Neither was his attempt to murder you. In my book, Skeeter owes you one."

"Call Rose quickly and make the arrangements, before I change my mind."

Ian winked. "I already have, and Kendall is willing to help us out. She's at the hospital now."

"Why is Rose and her entire extended family willing to help me?" Hannah asked.

"If you think you're repulsed by the idea of Skeeter being your father, it can't compare to how

Rose felt when she heard the news. I think she wants to get to the bottom of this almost as much as you do."

"Probably," Hannah agreed softly. But finding the truth now came with a price tag. It meant Ian would walk out of her life as quickly as he had walked in.

Hannah was glad he had left to change. Glad he couldn't see the single tear that slid down her cheek.

Chapter Thirteen

"He's O positive, you're AB negative," Dr. Kendall Revel said when she arrived at the Rose Tattoo and joined Hannah and Ian at one of the tables on the side porch later that day.

"What does that mean?" Hannah asked.

"Ten years ago, it would have excluded Mr. Pringle as your father. Now, we wait until the DNA results come back. They're more reliable."

Hannah thanked the doctor and looked at Ian as soon as they were alone. "I'm still stuck in maybe-land."

"Not really," Ian said. He shuffled through some of the documents they had brought over from Joanna's office. It had been Ian's suggestion, probably since being in the office had given Hannah the creeps. "Notice anything about these financial statements?"

"They're neat and organized."

"And," he said as he held two of them up in the sunlight, "they're all printed on paper with the same watermark."

"Skeeter could have provided me with copies," she suggested.

"With signed and dated original signatures on each one?"

They spent a few minutes comparing the documents. It was fairly obvious that they were as worthless as her phony birth certificate. "So what do you suggest I do?"

"Didn't Skeeter say he had three children?"

"That he knew of," Hannah answered with revulsion. "He also said he had a few ex-wives."

"Then," Ian began as he took her hand, "I think a trip to vital records is in order."

"Could we do something else first?" Hannah asked. When she saw the sensual curve of his mouth she said, "Not that."

"Sure?"

"I'm not sure of much of anything," she admitted. "But I'd like to go back to Magnolia Gardens. I just want to see if my memories of the place are real."

"Let's go."

Following the signs and Rose's hastily scribbled instructions, Ian and Hannah found the historic site with little difficulty. They parked and were greeted by a costumed employee who suggested they view the twelve-minute video on the plantation's history prior to wandering the area. They passed.

Hannah followed the path along the waterfowl refuge, somehow knowing that what she wanted was just beyond the petting zoo. She was right.

Three weathered benches guarded the entrance

to a horticultural maze. In the distance, she could see the observation towers for the bird-watchers and the antebellum cabin that was a hunting lodge for the original residents.

"It was here."

Ian was watching her with skepticism. "You seem pretty certain for someone who hasn't been here in more than twenty years.

"I'm telling you, this is where we would wait."

"Wait for what?" he asked.

Hannah sat on the bench, but that did nothing to jog her memory. "I don't know. I just know we always sat here, like we were waiting for something. Then Mother would go and talk to a man. That's all I can remember."

"Could the man have been Skeeter? It was a long time ago."

"Maybe I'm exaggerating his age, but I know the man had a different body type. He was tall and thin."

"Could it have been Dr. Longfellow?"

Hannah shook her head. "No. The man was taller than my father, and Dr. Longfellow is too short."

"What about Jeffrey Fielding?"

"I'd like to talk to him again," Hannah said. "I don't think it was him, but I wasn't paying close attention to him at the country club."

Ian checked his watch. "We'd better head back to town if we're going to check vital records before it closes. If we hurry, we can try to find Fielding's office, too."

When Hannah took the hand he held out to her, another memory jolted through her. "My mother never let go of my hand," she said. "Even when we would sit on the bench, she kept hold of me."

"Maybe she was just being cautious," Ian suggested.

"Maybe that's another *coincidence.*"

"I'VE GOT a third one," he whispered across the table to Hannah. "This one is a female child born the year before you."

"Same mother as the other two?" Hannah asked.

"Nope. That's three kids, one wife—Sarah Cummings Pringle, no divorce filed."

"She's probably at the hospital," Hannah suggested. "When did they marry?"

"Seventeen years ago. They had a son fifteen years ago, according to the state of South Carolina."

"What about the other two?"

Ian flipped back through his notepad. "The first one was a little girl, born thirty-two years ago, and the mother is listed as Tara Lynn Messner. Signed by our friend Dr. Longfellow."

"No record of Skeeter and Tara Lynn being married?"

He shook his head. "The second one was three years later, mother's name..." He looked up at Hannah and said, "Jane Smith. Signed by a Dr. Horace Vanderkemp."

"Gee, you don't think she put a false name on

the record, do you?'' she asked with a twinge of sarcasm.

''Let's focus on the first one,'' he suggested. ''Maybe she's never been married.''

''The chances of that are slim to none.''

He slipped his arm around her waist as they left the damp, musty basement. It felt so natural that he didn't stop to think; he just knew he wanted to touch her, to be close to her.

''Maybe his wife knows about his other children.''

''Do you want to go to intensive care, tap her on the shoulder and ask her if she's aware of any illegitimate children her husband has in the area?''

''Ouch,'' she said. ''That would be a little cold. Maybe Detective Ross can help us track her down.''

Ian steered her to the closest phone booth. ''Maybe we won't need Detective Ross's help.'' He glanced down at her mocking expression and smiled. ''Shall we wager?''

Her eyes narrowed accusingly. ''Something tells me I'm not going to like your terms.''

He feigned indignance. ''If I can locate Tara Lynn using one quarter and this phone book, you have to buy me dinner. If I can't, dinner is on me at the place of your choosing.''

''Deal. I hope I have something appropriate to wear to Carolina's,'' she purred. ''I hear the food is divine and the wine list exceptional. I also hear you can easily spend a couple of hundred dollars for dinner.''

"Thanks for the recommendation," Ian said as he flipped to the business section of the book. "I'll keep that in mind when I'm making my choice tonight."

He dropped his quarter into the phone and watched Hannah's smile fade when he asked to be put through to Special Agent Becker. After giving his friend the name and date of birth for Tara Lynn, he was forced to hold for at least five minutes before he had a current address for the woman.

He dangled it in front of Hannah's angry face. "The lady lives in Mount Pleasant."

"You cheated," she huffed.

"I used one quarter and the phone book. That was the deal."

"You called in some chit with one of your agency buddies. That wasn't playing fair. I could have done the same thing by calling Detective Ross."

When they reached the car, he looked down at her and asked, "Are you always such a poor loser?"

"Do you always cheat?"

"It's not cheating, it's expediting matters."

"Don't split hairs," she admonished. "I'll just hold on to the hope that you'll choke on whatever food I'm forced to buy you as a result of your sham of a bet."

He laughed. "You really are a sore loser, aren't you?"

"No." She sighed. "Just be gentle with me, Ian. Remember, I'm temporarily homeless and on leave from my job, but don't let that factor into your choice of restaurants."

"I won't. Is Carolina's really that good?"

"Yes."

"Pricey, too, you said?"

"Very."

"Do they have grilled sea bass on the menu? I really like grilled sea bass."

"I'm sure they'll have whatever you want."

"No," he pondered as he pulled into traffic. "Maybe a big filet would be better. Or maybe both. I've got a pretty healthy appetite."

"Geez, Ian! Enough. I'll make good on the bet."

He smiled. "That's all I wanted to hear."

Again aided by a map, Ian drove through some middle-class neighborhoods, then continued through housing that seemed to deteriorate with each passing mile. By the time they located Tara Lynn's address, they were in the middle of a field with two trailers parked dead center. One had fallen off its concrete blocks, so he led Hannah toward the one that looked livable—if one's definition of livable was generous.

A pair of mangy-looking dogs barked and jumped from a pen just to the right of the rusting structure. He wondered if the lopsided, handmade steps would hold his weight. Hannah must have had the same thought, because she brushed past him and reached through the tear in the screen to knock.

When the door opened, he smelled stale beer, stale smoke and grease. Those three things were far more pleasant than the look on the woman's face as she glared out at them. "Yeah?"

"Are you Tara Lynn Messner?" Hannah asked.

"Three marriages ago," she answered. "Unless you're here to give me the ten-million-dollar sweepstakes, I ain't interested."

"We aren't selling anything," Hannah assured the woman.

"Well then, I don't go to church, so let me get back to my show."

As she started to slam the door, Ian called to her. "Did you hear about Skeeter?"

The caution in her dark eyes turned to instant hatred. "No, and I'd be happy not to hear about him now."

"Please?" Hannah began.

Ian ventured onto the bottom step. "He tried to kill this lady last night."

Tara Lynn didn't bat an eye. "Skeeter's good at killing things."

"May we come in?" Ian asked.

Tara Lynn stepped from inside the trailer and led them to a collection of mismatched, rusted chairs beneath a live oak draped with moss. "Hush up!" she called to the dogs as she took a cigarette out of a crumpled pack and lit it, drawing deeply before asking, "Why did you come to me?"

"Skeeter and I might be...related," Hannah answered.

"We think that's why he tried to kill her," Ian added.

"I didn't know Skeeter cared enough about his

kids to bother with killing one,'' Tara Lynn said to Hannah.

''He's not close with your daughter?''

Tara Lynn laughed, which quickly turned into one of those coughing fits that proclaim a lifelong addiction to nicotine. ''That would be a trick, now, wouldn't it?''

''I don't understand,'' Hannah said.

''You think I wanted to end up like this?'' she said, waving her hands in an arc around her dreary surroundings. ''I thought Skeeter was my ticket to the easy life. 'Course I was eighteen and stupid at the time.''

''You and Skeeter were...?'' Hannah left the inference dangling.

''You bet. Him *and* his friend Jeffrey. *And* about three other guys, too. Hell, I was giving it away back in those days. I smartened up after I had the kid.''

Ian didn't think Tara sounded like mother of the year, but then he figured her current life-style was probably punishment enough. ''You got pregnant?''

''Sure did,'' Tara Lynn answered. ''Course I couldn't have told you who the father was.''

''So you just picked Skeeter's name for the birth certificate?''

She shook her head. ''Nope. I picked Skeeter because I figured he was the only one of them snooty men who might do right by me.''

''Snooty men?'' Ian repeated.

''You know. Born with money and no responsibilities. The whole lot of them can burn in hell.''

"How did you meet Skeeter?"

"Through work," Tara Lynn said. "He used to be a fairly decent-looking man. He paid for me to have an apartment when my papa threw me out. Paid all my medical bills." Her face grew sad for a minute before the toughness returned. "I shoulda known he wasn't in it for the long haul when he hemmed and hawed about getting married."

"Did Skeeter know there were other...possible fathers?" Hannah asked.

Tara Lynn shrugged. "He knew my reputation. But he never did ask, which is why I stupidly hung on to the belief that he would marry me."

"Where is your daughter now?" Ian asked.

Tara Lynn's face transformed. The harsh, abrasive almost combative expression drained away along with her color. "She's dead."

Ian reached out and gripped Hannah's hand. "Did Skeeter—"

"Those doctors screwed up. I'm sure I heard her tiny cry in the delivery room. But they gave me drugs. Next thing I know some other doctor is at my bedside in the ward telling me she didn't make it. Some sort of heart defect."

"How did Skeeter take it?"

Tara Lynn took another long drag, then blew out a steady stream of smoke. "I wouldn't know. I left the hospital, the landlady told me I had one week to get out and there was a note from Skeeter telling me he had had the baby cremated. I haven't talked to the bastard since."

"I'm sorry," Hannah said. "I had no idea your

baby had died. I wouldn't have bothered you if—"

"It was a long time ago," she said, then gave a small chuckle. "I was hurting after that doctor told me my baby was gone, but I was mad when they gave me that birth certificate to fill out. I put his name on it out of spite. It was hard enough knowing she had died, but filling out all that paperwork with that box marked Stillborn on it was probably the hardest thing I ever had to do."

Ian and Hannah rose in unison, leaving Tara Lynn to her pathetic life and sad memories. As they reached the car, Ian thought of something, turned and called Tara Lynn's name.

"What?"

"Did you work at one of the dealerships? Is that how you knew Skeeter and his friends?"

"No. I cleaned at the club."

"The Oyster Point Society?" he asked.

"Yes."

"I feel sorry for her," Hannah said as soon as they were back in the car. "What a horrible way to live."

"It's worse than you think," Ian said.

"How could anything be worse than losing a child?"

Ian ignored the stab of pain in his chest. "Reach in the back and get the copy of the birth certificate for Tara Lynn's baby."

He waited while she read it, then he heard her sharp intake of breath. "Her baby wasn't stillborn."

Chapter Fourteen

"I want soup and salad," he said as he parked in front of the condo. "And I'd like you to prepare it."

Hannah winced. "I don't cook."

"How hard is soup and a salad?" he argued. "I won the bet, I have decided that I'd like a nice home-cooked meal."

"Then go home and cook one," she griped.

"Be a gracious loser." He swatted her on the fanny as they entered the building. Of course, the prune-faced manager Mrs. Wilkerson had to be there to witness the little scene.

Her disgusted reaction just caused them both to laugh like naughty schoolchildren as they rode the elevator to the top floor.

Hannah surveyed the contents of the refrigerator and managed to find enough things to put together a salad. Ian had opened a bottle of wine and seemed content just to watch her struggle through the task of cutting radishes, slicing carrots and tearing lettuce. By the time she had finished,

Hannah had a nick in her fingers from the blade of the knife.

"Don't bleed on my food," Ian warned.

Hannah looked up at him as she made another bandage from a strip of napkin. "There's no soup."

"Then you'd better run to the market before it closes. I'm partial to chicken noodle."

"I'd rather run you down," she grumbled as she grabbed her purse and started out the door.

"You might want to think about buying some bandages. Maybe a burn kit if you're going to use the stove."

"Very funny, MacPhearson," she said, though she couldn't keep the smile from her eyes. "Maybe I can find a dented can of soup. I heard there's a chance of getting botulism if the can's dented."

She made it out the door just as one of the cushions from the sofa hit the wall. Her trip to the market took a little longer than expected. It wasn't that she was a poor shopper, it was more like she was used to her own store and, even then, she only frequented two aisles—junk food and frozen dinners. She went to the bakery and grabbed a loaf of freshly baked bread, then grabbed a fruit pie just for good measure.

When she returned, she found that Ian had set the table, dimmed the lights and figured out how to work the stereo system that had more lights, knobs and buttons than the space shuttle.

"Two bags for soup?" he teased as he came and took the heavier sack from her. "I see. You went to the store hungry and made several impulse purchases. Not a very thrifty way to live."

"I'm still spending less than it would have cost you *if* you would have played fair."

He came up behind her, reaching over her shoulder to help unpack the items. "I can do this myself," she snapped.

"I was only trying to help."

"Rubbing up against me isn't helping. It's distracting."

"I see," he murmured as his lips brushed her ear. His fingers played across her stomach as he nuzzled her neck. "And what happens if I do this?"

His teeth nibbled at her earlobe. Hannah was suddenly reduced to a quivering mass of raging hormones. Still no need to tell him that. "Absolutely nothing."

He let out a deep, throaty chuckle. "What about this?" he asked as his palms inched higher until the tips of his fingers were dangerously close to her breasts. At the same time, his lips seared kisses against her cheek. "Still nothing?" he murmured softly.

"Dinner will be a little late," she said as she turned in his arms and gave him a dose of his own medicine.

This wasn't like the first time. Though their need for each other was still intense, this was slower, more playful and incredibly intimate.

"You're smiling," she said later as she grabbed her shirt and started to dress.

"I'm supposed to smile. So are you."

"I'm smiling," she said as she turned away from him.

"No, you aren't."

Hannah kept her back to him as she dressed. She heard the rustle of fabric that told her he was slipping into his jeans. "Hannah?"

When she turned and looked up into his expressive eyes, she wanted to cry and laugh all at once. It was as if someone had thrown her emotions into a blender and everything was garbled. "I'm just miffed because I still have soup to make," she lied as she pulled away from him.

She managed to open the can without doing great bodily harm to herself. Actually, she was rather pleased with her effort when she placed the meager meal on the table. "As you wished," she said. "Thank Piggly Wiggly for the bread and the pie. Believe me, it has to be far better than anything I could ever whip up."

She looked across the table at him—his hair was mussed, his shirt unbuttoned. Instead of marveling at the glorious thing they had shared, all she could think about was the reality that it was only temporary.

"Ask me."

"Ask you what?" she returned, genuinely confused.

"I don't know, but you look like you're about to be sacrificed to the lions."

"Cooking doesn't agree with me," she answered, hoping to turn the conversation to a lighter note.

"You were right about one thing."

"I can't cook?"

His eyes held hers. "You aren't a very good liar."

She nodded. "Okay. I suppose I have given a thought or two to how I'm going to walk away from you."

"Meaning?"

Hannah rolled her eyes. "No hidden meaning. I didn't come here expecting to find someone like you. I like being with you and it's only natural that, given that fact, it will be a little hard for me to say goodbye to you."

He dropped his spoon with a clang and the look in his eyes told her volumes.

"I said hard, not *impossible,*" she added, feeling defensive and hurt.

"I was responsible for another person once in my life, Hannah, I don't think I could handle it again."

Defensiveness grew into anger. "How convenient to be the grieving widower *after* you have sex with me."

"I never meant for you to take it like that," he began.

Hannah stood so quickly that her chair fell back and hit the floor. "I won't have this discussion with you. Let's just agree that we'll refrain from recreational sex, because I'm not into a threesome."

"What the hell is that supposed to mean?" he thundered.

"It's a little crowded with you, me and your dead wife. If your loyalties are to a memory, fine,

I can respect that." Hannah was so emotional she was actually trembling. "And just for the record, I'm not mad at you, I'm mad at myself. I went into this with my eyes wide-open. I just didn't see where I was going. I've lost my appetite."

"No, ma'am," he said as he grabbed her arm. "Maybe the other people in your life let you get away with your hit-and-run approach to an argument, but not me."

She glared up at him. "We aren't having an argument."

"Yes, we are. And you're going to sit down and participate in it."

Hannah let out a heavy sigh. "Why, Ian? So you can tell me how guilty you feel for telling your wife you didn't love her and wanted a divorce and then she died? I already know all that."

He looked down at her, his eyes glistening. "No. So I can tell you that on the day Carmen died she told me she was pregnant. I told her I didn't want her to keep working. She basically told me to go to hell, it was her career. I told her it was her career or our marriage."

Hannah pulled him into her arms and pulled his head to her shoulder. They remained like that for several moments, until Ian turned and walked to the guest room and slammed the door. Only then did Hannah reach up and feel the wetness his silent tears had left on her shoulder.

She waited a long time to see if he would come back. He didn't, and she knew then that it was over. She couldn't compete with a ghost or all that guilt. At least she knew exactly where she stood with him. All she had to do now was find some way to stop loving him.

THE NEXT MORNING they were very careful not to make contact. It seemed as if they had separately come to the same conclusion.

"Fancy digs," Hannah commented as she and Ian entered the offices of Fielding and MacBride, Attorneys at Law. Even the reception area was posh, complete with leather sofas, antiques and gilded mirrors.

"May I help you?" a pretty blonde asked as she peered over the lenses of half glasses.

"I'd like to see Mr. Fielding," Hannah said.

Her request was greeted with a frown. "Do you have an appointment?"

"No. I met Mr. Fielding at the charity golf function last weekend, and I just wanted to pay a social call."

"Wait here," she said, then disappeared behind a door marked Private.

"We aren't getting in," Hannah whispered to Ian.

"How do you know that?"

"Because 'wait here' is law office lingo for 'when pigs fly.'"

Ian wandered around the spacious office, reading the various awards, diplomas, certificates of appreciation and news clippings that hung between mirrors and original oil paintings. "Well, well," she heard him mutter.

Moving next to him, she looked at the article, then read the identifying lines beneath the two men. "Past presidents of the Oyster Point Society, Jeffrey Fielding and Colton Mays. Think Mays might be the third man Dr. Longfellow couldn't recall?"

"Yep."

"It says he's the director of the local arts council. He shouldn't be too hard to track down."

As Hannah had predicted, the receptionist returned with an insincere apology and basically told them to go away.

"That was a waste of time," Ian grumbled.

"Not really. I got a look at Colton Mays. I don't think he's the man I remember, either."

"We're running out of possibilities," Ian stated. "I'm hungry. Feel like mooching off Rose again?"

"Sure," Hannah agreed quickly. At least at the Rose Tattoo she could surround herself with people and not have to watch her every word and movement. Besides, Rose was always friendly, and she was definitely in the mood for a friend.

Apparently, Rose was, too. "Thankfully, someone who can help!" she called through the crowd of patrons lined up at the bar.

"I've been calling Joleen for an hour. This isn't like her. Would you mind going over to her place to see if she's okay?"

"Of course," Hannah and Ian said in unison.

Rose's green eyes narrowed. "We're backed up, and I really need her to get her butt in here." Rose paused, then added as an afterthought, "If she is okay, kill her."

Following the directions given by Rose, Ian and

Hannah drove to a part of the city that probably never makes it into the tourist guides. "This can't be right," Hannah said as they parked on a side street where houses had boarded-up windows, graffiti and trash strewn about.

Hannah heard the sounds of something scattering about when they ventured inside, and she figured they were rats—she just didn't dare look to confirm it. The building smelled of garbage and urine, and Hannah again said, "We must have gotten the directions wrong."

Then she saw the name scratched above the mailbox—Joleen Hawkins.

"Either Rose pays slave wages or Joleen has a mental block about spending money," Ian observed as they climbed to the second floor. He knocked twice, and when he got no response, he used a credit card to jimmy the lock.

"You're breaking and entering," Hannah accused.

"I'm checking on a friend," he whispered. In the shadows, Hannah saw a figure and let out a little scream.

Ian pushed her behind him, but the shadow didn't move. Hannah felt along the wall behind her, found the switch and flipped it.

"It isn't real," she said as she looked at the form. "None of this stuff is real," she added as she scanned the strange surroundings. The tenement was filled with sculptures in all shapes and sizes. They were beautiful and carved from expensive stones. "At least we know how she spends her money," Hannah observed.

They checked the adjoining bedroom, and Hannah knew instantly that Joleen had left voluntarily.

"How can you be so sure?" he challenged.

"No makeup in the bathroom, no undergarments in the drawers and there are several empty hangers in her closet."

"And twenty-five grand in the bank," Ian added.

"What?" Hannah said as she came to read the statement in his hand. "For less than a day," she said. "Look, the bank did a debit the afternoon the money was deposited. Talk about bank error in your favor."

He met her eyes. "I'm sensing coincidence again."

"Look at the date," she said, tapping the page with her finger. "The money was deposited after my parents died, so it can't have anything to do with them. And it was before I came to Charleston, so I doubt Skeeter would be laundering money through her. Besides, my parents only paid in five-thousand-dollar increments."

"Then where is she?"

The phone rang and Hannah assumed it would be Rose asking for a report. On the seventh ring, she figured Joleen didn't have a machine, so she lifted the receiver and said, "Hello?"

"Get out of town. Now."

"Hello?"

"Now, or you'll die."

Ian must have sensed something was wrong because he immediately rushed to her side. "What?"

Hannah replaced the receiver and repeated the conversation. "Warning was more like it."

"I have a hard time picturing someone threatening Joleen. I haven't heard the woman utter six words since I met her."

Hannah peered up at him; her throat was dry and her chest was tight. "He meant me."

Ian's brows drew together. "We haven't been followed since Skeeter stroked out. Detective Ross has already matched paint chips from your rental car to a car at one of Skeeter's dealerships. They would have notified us if Skeeter was out of the coma."

She gripped his sleeve as the room began to spin. "I recognized the voice."

"Who was it?"

Chapter Fifteen

"I know I was only five, but I'm telling you for the umpteenth time, it was the same man," Hannah insisted as they entered through the back of the Rose Tattoo.

Things appeared to be running more smoothly, though Hannah also noticed two of the evening waiters had arrived. She smiled at DeLancey, the new chef, then slipped up the stairs in search of Rose.

"I'm assuming she'll have a good explanation," Rose said without preamble. "What is wrong with you?" she said as her eyes washed over Hannah.

"Nothing, really. What do you know about Joleen?" she asked.

Rose shrugged. "She's been here about a year. This is the first time she's ever pulled a stunt like this. Lord, Hannah! You're as white as a sheet."

"I got a call when we were at Joleen's apartment—if you can call it that."

Ian described what they had found, while Hannah sat in one of the chairs and calmed her nerves. "I know I recognized that voice."

"But how would anyone know you'd be at Joleen's apartment?" Rose argued. "Some people sound alike on the phone."

Hannah raised her hand. "Okay, fine. I'm delusional. Then explain to me why Skeeter Pringle would want to kill me and why some woman named Tara Lynn Messner thinks she had a stillbirth, when we even went back to check and there's no death certificate. What else?" Hannah shoved her hair out of her eyes. "Oh, yes, there's the fact that my parents paid their life savings to someone thirty-one years ago and I suddenly materialized; then five years later they drained themselves financially by sending cashier's checks to a post office box here in Charleston." She looked at Rose. "And all I know is my birth certificate is phony and you somehow tie into all this."

Rose fell into her seat, opened a drawer, pulled out three glasses and poured them each a drink. "I'm not the link, Hannah. If I knew anything that would help you, believe me, I'd come clean."

"I do believe you. I just know that it is probably something obvious and I'm not seeing it."

"The lapel pin," Ian said.

Hannah nodded and looked at Rose. "Does the name Colton Mays mean anything to you?"

She laughed without humor. "Yes, it means I'm expected to write a check."

"Blackmail?"

"Arts council," Rose answered. "He's always hitting up the downtown businesses to sponsor one event or another. He owns a fancy gallery over on Meeting Street.''

Hannah looked to Ian. ''Maybe he's the one who called me?''

''Would you say the man had a deep, menacing tone?'' Rose asked.

''Yes.''

''Then it wasn't Colton Mays.''

''How can you be so sure?'' Hannah asked.

Rose gave a wicked grin. ''He's discreet, and I've never seen it mentioned in the society column, but Colton butters his bread on the wrong side.''

''He's gay?''

Rose nodded. ''I don't really care what the man does in his own home with consenting adults. The funny part is, he's the only one who doesn't seem to know it's the worst-kept secret in Charleston.'' Rose tossed back the rest of her drink. ''I hate to generalize, but the man is extremely effeminate. His voice is about as deep and menacing as Tinkerbell's.''

''Joleen had a bunch of sculptures in her apartment. Is there a chance she might be connected to Colton Mays?'' Ian asked.

''I don't see how,'' Rose answered. ''Joleen and Colton don't exactly travel in the same social circles.'' Rose frowned suddenly. ''In fact, every time Colton sashays in here for another handout, Joleen usually hides in the back until he's gone. I just figured she didn't care for his sexual orientation.''

Hannah and Ian looked at each other. "Colton Mays," they said in unison.

Just as they were about to leave, Rose got a call and motioned for them to stay. "I'll tell her, and thanks."

"Kendall got the initial DNA results back. Luckily for you, Skeeter Pringle is not your father."

They decided to walk the few short blocks to Meeting Street. Hannah focused on their silhouettes as they walked side by side on the uneven sidewalk. Like New Orleans, the walkways were slanted to force rainwater into the streets. "All they need are a few sex shops and a voodoo shop and this would be like home."

"I know."

She peered up at him. "You've been to New Orleans."

He nodded. "A few times."

"And?"

"It's crowded."

She smiled. "That's what makes it fun and exciting. There's always something going on."

"I know. Pickpockets, carjackings—uumppp." He groaned when she elbowed his rib cage. "I apologize, but you've got to admit, living in a city does come with its fair share of crime."

"I suppose Podunk, Montana, is crime free?"

"I live in Brock's Pass, not Podunk."

"Sounds like a happening town," Hannah teased. "Let me guess, a drive-in, a luncheonette with Formica counters, one filling station and about twelve churches."

He laughed. "Very good, but I think there are only eleven churches, and you forgot the general store."

"Sorry," she said with a sigh. "It's just been a while since I saw a rerun of 'Father Knows Best.'"

"Don't knock the simple life until you've tried it," he said as he reached for the polished brass handle of the Mays Gallery.

There were maybe three other couples and two single patrons strolling through the long, narrow gallery. Paintings hung on the walls and the center of the room held sculptures and blown-glass pieces with nothing more than titles and the name of the artist.

"No price tags," Hannah whispered. "That normally means I can't afford it."

"It normally means I don't like it," Ian whispered back as they came upon a rusted, twisted piece of metal mounted on a granite base. "Hell, I've got some old truck parts that look like this."

"Hush," she urged as they continued to browse. "That's pretty," she commented when she spotted a delicate, single rose crafted of glass and decorated with some sort of enameled finish.

"Want it?"

She gave him a quick glare. "I'm homeless, remember. Besides, I'd probably break it before I got it back to New Orleans and that's just assuming I could afford the asking price."

His expression grew serious. "Are you in trouble financially?"

She smiled, touched by his concern. "I'm gainfully employed, and I've got enough saved to tide me over until I get back to work. Rose's letting me stay in the condo has really helped."

"I could—"

Her look stopped him in mid-sentence. "I really won't starve to death, and the only reason I'm homeless is because I didn't bother to look for an apartment before I came here. It seemed silly to pay rent when I knew I could be gone for a while."

"You've convinced me."

"Then you've decided?" a gentleman said as he approached. "That is a lovely piece, excellent craftsmanship. The artist spent ten years in Florence studying with some of the best glassblowers in the world."

"Ian MacPhearson," he said as he offered his hand.

Though the man tried to hide it, there was a flicker of recognition in his eyes. "I'm Colton Mays."

Apparently, Ian didn't miss it, either. "Which one of your Oyster Point Society buddies warned you we'd be by?"

"Perhaps we should continue this conversation in my office," he suggested. On the way through the gallery, Mays stopped and instructed a well-groomed man to handle things and to hold his calls.

Hannah recognized the surroundings—at least, she recognized the taste. "You decorated Jeffrey Fielding's offices, didn't you?"

"Yes, among many others here in town. My

decorating business is really just a hobby," he said as small beads of sweat formed above his upper lip. "You're the young woman Pringle is accused of attacking, am I correct?"

Hannah watched the nervous little man closely. "Yes, and I was hoping you might be able to tell me why."

"Me?" Mays asked with a flip of the scarf he had draped over the lapels of his designer suit. "I haven't kept in touch with Mr. Pringle."

"Why not?" Ian asked. "Dr. Longfellow said you were pretty tight when you first joined the Oyster Point Society."

"Mr. Pringle was allowed membership because his grandfather had been a member. That is in our charter. We had no way of refusing him."

"So you never liked the guy?" Ian pressed. "Is that what you're saying?"

The perspiration now encompassed his forehead, as well. "I didn't dislike him—we simply weren't well suited for friendship."

"Then Dr. Longfellow is lying?"

"Of course not," Mays responded quickly. "The three of us were the only new members brought in that year. We were together some of the time simply because we were of a common age."

"Since Skeeter isn't in any position to dial a phone, my guess is it was Fielding who called you."

"I've been in Europe on a buying trip," Mays answered. "I only returned yesterday, and I happened to run into Jeffrey. He mentioned this latest scandal."

"Latest scandal?" Hannah repeated. "Skeeter has done this sort of thing before?"

"I really wouldn't know," Mays insisted as he walked to the door. "I'm afraid I must ask you to leave now. I do have a business to run."

"Thanks for your time," Ian said as he placed his hand on her back.

It remained there until they left the building, then Hannah quickened her pace so that he had no choice but to stop touching her.

"Well?"

"It wasn't his voice and I *know* he wasn't the man I remember from the garden trips."

"What now?"

"The fire stairs."

"Excuse me?"

"You said we could get into the Oyster Point Society by using the fire stairs."

"You said it was illegal."

"So is selling babies from unsuspecting mothers," Hannah said. "Now it's more important to me to know how I was adopted rather than who my parents are."

"There's always the possibility that there is a death certificate for Tara Lynn's baby and it was just misfiled."

"Aren't you the one always harping about coincidences?"

"That I am," he agreed. "I guess it can't hurt to take a look around. But I think I should go alone."

"Wrong. We're going together."

Ian stopped her in the center of the sidewalk. "I have friends who can get me out of it if I get caught."

"And I'll plead temporary insanity brought on by Skeeter's attempt on my life and represent myself." She shrugged away from his hold. "Now that we've decided how we'll cover our respective rear ends, explain to me how we do this."

"I CAN'T BELIEVE you made me wait so long," she grumbled as he pulled her through the second-story window.

"By watching last night, I knew what time the caretaker left. I also know that we have about a two-hour window before the cleaning people arrive."

"What about alarms?"

"I took care of that," he told her. When she gave him a blank stare, he said, "I cut the wires and did a dry run last night, just to see if there was a silent alarm."

"What did you find?"

"Nothing, but let's start downstairs."

"Why?"

"Because we want to be near our escape route if someone should come in."

"Oh. You really did learn a few useful things in secret-agent school, didn't you?"

"I learned to be quiet when I was trespassing."

"Sorry."

He held firmly to her hand as they began to descend the staircase. They were only on the second step when he felt Hannah jerk to a stop and make a strangled sound.

"That's him!" she said as she pointed her flashlight on the portrait. "That's the man from the gardens!"

Ian turned his light on the brass plate beneath the painting. "Horace Vanderkemp, M.D. The same doctor that signed the birth certificate for Jane Smith's baby."

"He's the president now," Hannah said excitedly. "Which means he probably has an office."

Ian turned and went back up, taking Hannah with him. "I seem to remember a door with his name on it."

Ian made quick work of the flimsy lock and the two of them entered the office and looked around. Nothing that connected Vanderkemp to Skeeter was obvious, so he suggested she check the desk and he took the filing cabinet.

"He's generous," Hannah whispered. "Or rather the Society is. They must write a dozen checks a month to different charities. They're planning on having the senator speak at their next luncheon. I hope you're finding more interesting stuff than I am."

His eyes scanned the document in his hand, then he folded it and waited until he was sure she was distracted before he slipped it inside his shirt. He continued looking through the records.

"This is pointless." Hannah sighed. "I have a letter here with his home address. I say we go over and pay a house call on the doctor."

Ian nodded. As he turned, he thought he heard

a sound from below. He went still, as did Hannah, who must have heard it, as well. Using only hand signals, he had her turn off her flashlight and they moved to the fire stairs. As he was closing the window, Ian saw the silhouette of a man at the far end of the hall. If they were lucky, the man hadn't seen them.

"Quickly," he said as he grabbed Hannah's hand and half dragged her to the wall, then practically tossed her over it before scaling it himself. He looked back once, relieved when he saw no signs of whoever had been in the building.

DR. VANDERKEMP LIVED on an estate near the outskirts of Charleston overlooking the river. "Apparently, he's been living the good life," Hannah remarked. "Maybe that good life is the result of God knows how many people he's been blackmailing."

"Let's try talking to the man first," Ian suggested. "Assuming we can roust anyone at this hour."

"I'm sure the doctor is in. There's a Bentley in the driveway."

The third time they rang the ornate buzzer, a half-awake butler answered the door. He frowned at Ian, then when he looked at Hannah he said, "Miss Hillary, how nice to see you. What are you doing out and about at this time of night?"

He took her elbow as if she were some hundred-year-old maiden aunt. "Hannah," she said loudly. "I want to see Dr. Vanderkemp now."

"Of course, you do. I'll go and fetch him, you just sit right here," he said.

Hannah sat until the man left the room, then walked toward the fireplace and admired a woman in a large portrait hanging above it. Then she happened to catch a glimpse out the double doors. "Look at this," she said to Ian.

He moved over and followed her line of sight. Small spotlights illuminated sculptures that seemed to match the design and feel of the ones they had seen at Joleen's apartment.

"The woman waits tables when she can sculpt and has the good doctor as a patron?" Hannah wondered. "Or maybe the good doctor sculpts and has Joleen as a—"

"I've been expecting you."

Ian watched the recognition in her eyes as she turned and faced the tall, dignified man with the shock of white hair.

"You called me," Hannah said in a near whisper.

"I'm sorry you didn't heed my warning, Miss Bailey," he said as he held firmly to the lapels of his robe. "It isn't a good idea for you to stay in Charleston. You've put a great many lives in danger."

Ian placed his arm around her, not quite sure how she would react when and if the doctor told her the truth. "I'm Ian MacPhearson," he said. "She's a little volatile, so you might want to tell her the truth."

"I remember you," Hannah began before the doctor could speak. "Was that part of the deal?

You sold me like a commodity and then checked on your investment?"

"I wasn't the one who—"

Ian heard the shot, and his first instinct was to toss Hannah behind the sofa. "Stay down!" he shouted as he pulled a gun from inside his ankle holster and stepped through the now-shattered doors into the garden.

Hannah crawled toward Vanderkemp at the same moment the butler reappeared. "Call the police and an ambulance. He's still alive!"

Ian! Hannah spotted the gun rack and yanked the first rifle she put her hands on. "Is it loaded?" she wondered aloud as she bent the barrel. "Hurry," she mumbled to herself as she found a box of shells and loaded the rifle, then followed Ian into the garden.

Between the spotlights, shadows and sculptures, Hannah had a hard time focusing on what was real and what wasn't. She pointed her weapon at anything and everything, but didn't dare fire. The garden was a maze of plants, trees and fountains, so she couldn't depend on her sense of hearing for help. She was just about to enter a pathway by one of the fountains when she saw him. Ian had his back to her. He also had his back to the arms she saw protruding from behind one of the statues. The arms had a gun pointed right at Ian.

Lifting the gun toward the statue, she yelled, "Ian!" then squeezed the trigger at the same time she heard another gun go off.

"HE'S POSITIVE?" Hannah asked.

Detective Ross handed her a cup of coffee as their interview moved into the dawn. "Fielding was your father. Apparently, Skeeter owed him a favor, but when Skeeter had his stroke, Fielding decided to do it himself."

"What about my mother? Did the doctor tell you her name before they took him into surgery?"

The detective shook his head. "All we got from Vanderkemp before he went under was that he had arranged the adoption for Fielding. He mentioned doing the same thing for Skeeter."

"Tell that to Tara Lynn Messner," Hannah said, then explained her meeting with the woman.

"I guess we'll have to wait until Vanderkemp is out of surgery before we can get the rest of the story."

Hannah nodded and thanked him. "Is it okay if Ian takes me home now?"

The detective seemed puzzled. "Ian left several hours ago. But Rose is out there."

"You look like hell," Rose said when they met in the hall.

"Would you believe I look better than I feel?" Hannah tried her best to smile.

"I'm sorry about your father."

"Andrew Bailey was my father," Hannah said with conviction. "Fielding was just a sperm donor."

"You'll feel better once you get some rest."

"Is Ian at the condo?"

"No."

Hearing that bit of news was all it took to send

her into tears. "I'm sorry. I guess I should have seen this coming."

"He hasn't left town. If you ask me, he won't until he sees this through to the end."

"Last night was the end."

Hannah felt alone and lonely for the first time when Rose dropped her off. The condo seemed empty and huge without Ian there. She was bone tired, but she couldn't fall asleep. Then she went into the guest room, took one of his shirts from the closet, slipped it on and felt comforted by his scent.

That was how Ian found her later that day. He wasn't prepared to walk in on her, balled in a fetal position, wearing his shirt. He closed his eyes, hating himself for what he had done and what he was about to do.

"Hannah?"

She awoke with a start. The moment her eyes focused, she smiled at him. "Hi."

"I need you to get dressed."

He saw the raw emotion in her eyes but knew there was no other way to handle this. "I'll be in the guest room if you need anything."

"I'm fine."

Ian was folding the last of his clothes into his suitcase when she appeared at the door. "I can have it laundered and sent to you," she suggested as she held out the shirt of his she had been wearing.

"I'll take it back like that."

They stared at each other for a long moment,

then Hannah—simply, quietly and honestly—said, "I love you."

He thought his chest would burst from the pain of hearing her say those words. "I killed your father."

"We don't know that, and I made Detective Ross promise me he would never tell me which one of us fired the fatal shot."

"It won't work, Hannah."

"Because you don't love me?"

"Because I came within an inch of watching you die. I don't want to go through that again."

She nodded. "So I guess we say goodbye."

"Not yet."

She held up her hand. "Look, I pretty much used up all my nerve telling you I loved you when I was pretty sure it was a long shot. Your wife wasn't the only one that died five years ago. The only difference is, you didn't crawl in the grave with her. I'm sorry for you, Ian. I think I'm more sorry for you than I am for myself."

He was amazed at the way she maintained her composure. He would have felt better if she'd rushed up and slapped him. "There's someone I want you to meet."

"I think the sooner we part ways, the better."

"I agree. But I would appreciate it if you would do me this one favor."

"Which is?"

"You're just going to have to trust me."

"When haven't I?"

In his car, she sat next to him in the physical sense, but Hannah was keenly aware of how important it was to keep her dignity, or what was left of it. They were just south of Columbia when Ian turned off the highway.

A few more miles and they came to the entrance for the Fairhaven School for the Deaf and Blind. Her heart was broken, but her mind was still functioning. "You found my mother."

He nodded as they drove up a beautifully landscaped driveway to a huge building with flower boxes and childish paintings taped to the windows.

"Does she teach here?" Hannah asked as she jumped from the car before he had completely stopped.

"Hang on!" he yelled.

She ignored him, but he caught up with her by the third step. When Hannah opened the door, she was greeted by a woman whose smile froze in place.

"Hello?" she said. "I'm Hannah Bailey."

"Good gracious" the woman muttered, shaking her head. "This way," she said as she led Hannah down a hallway. Every now and then, the woman would look back at Hannah with a puzzled expression on her face. Hannah figured she probably looked like her mother.

"Go right in," the lady said, indicating the closed door. Then Hannah walked into a studio.

At the opposite end of the room, Joleen sat on a chair next to a young woman who was Hannah's mirror image except for a different hairstyle.

"Who?" the woman asked.

When she turned in Hannah's direction, it was

immediately apparent from her speech and her movement that the woman was deaf and blind. "Who?" she demanded impatiently in barely understandable English.

Joleen took the woman's hand and signed something. Then the woman smiled. "Yes?"

"What is this?" Hannah asked. "What's going on?"

Joleen came forward with her head bowed and Hannah's twin on her elbow. "Mr. MacPhearson thought you would want to know the truth."

Hannah was staring openly now. "Which is what?"

"This is your sister."

"I gathered that from the resemblance."

Joleen stopped for a minute to sign into Hannah's sister's hand. Whatever was communicated seemed to calm the impatience she sensed. "I had twins when I was sixteen." Joleen lifted her head and met Hannah's gaze. "They were both beautiful, but one was deaf, blind and mildly retarded. The man who got me pregnant had a list of friends willing to claim they had slept with me, too, so a paternity suit wasn't an option. The doctor told me that if I would agree to give up the perfect baby, he would make sure I had everything I needed to care for the other."

Hannah drew her bottom lip in between her teeth to keep from crying.

"He promised me that the family who took you would love you and give you everything you would ever need. The social worker said it would be best if I gave you both up. They wanted me to put Hillary in some warehouse for the mentally ill. So I did what I thought was best for both of you. I didn't know until you showed up at the Rose Tattoo that Fielding had been paid, or that he had been blackmailing your family. I guess that's why they stopped bringing you here. We had agreed that I could watch you grow up, so long as I did it from a distance. I would sit in the observation tower at Magnolia Gardens and watch you. Then they just stopped coming."

"How did Rose's name get on my birth certificate?"

"I saw a picture of her in the newspaper. It was the same New Year's Eve picture that Mr. MacPhearson found."

"Why didn't you say something when I first showed up?"

"Jeffrey Fielding was a powerful man. He warned me that you were coming and that if any of this became public, he'd make sure this institution lost its funding. This is Hillary's home." Joleen dropped her head as tears streamed down her face. "For the second time I felt I had to protect her. She sculpts and she draws and she's happy here. I knew after that first meeting that you were strong enough to take care of yourself. I think I took the job working for Rose secretly hoping that you might come looking for me one day. You must really hate me."

"No," Hannah whispered. "I'm really glad to meet you. Both of you."

Epilogue

A month later, Hannah opened the door to the condo and found Joleen on the doorstep. "Can you believe I'm still packing?" she asked. "Come on in."

"You have to hurry."

"My plane isn't for another two hours."

"We have to go by the Rose Tattoo."

Hannah pressed her fingers to her temples. "We only left there six hours ago. I think I overdid the wine at the party."

"We have to. Hillary did a special sculpture for Rose, and I want you to see it before you leave."

"Okay, but how did you make Hillary understand Elvis? Did she do young Elvis or old Elvis?"

"Just hurry," Joleen said.

"Where is it?" she asked a short time later when Joleen pulled up at the rear entrance.

"In Rose's office."

Hannah walked alone to the back door and entered, surprised when she saw none of the normal activity. She didn't wear a watch, but she knew they should have been gearing up for lunch. "I must be more hungover than I thought."

"I hope not," a man's voice said.

"Ian?" she asked cautiously, not trusting her own ears.

"In here."

She stood in the doorway of the office, which was arranged as it had been the night Joleen had brought them dinner. The night they had shared their first kiss.

"What is this?"

"Lunch?" he suggested innocently.

She searched his face. "Look, if you came back to say a proper goodbye, it isn't necessary."

"It isn't?"

"No."

"What if I came for another reason?"

The devilish light in his eyes gave her hope, but she remained cautious. "Depends on the reason."

"Well," he said, stroking his chin for effect. "I have a gourmet meal for two."

"That's nice."

"I have flowers for you."

"Also nice."

"I have a vintage wine chilled."

"Usually that would be nice."

"I have a ring," he said, slipping his hand into his pocket and retrieving a velvet box. When he opened the hinged lid, she almost gasped at the size of the diamond.

"That's *very* nice."

"Since you haven't come racing into my arms, I must have forgotten something."

"Yes, you did."

"I love you, Hannah."

"That's nice."

He seemed genuinely perplexed. "Okay, what did I forget?"

"You tell me?"

He was quiet for a moment, then a huge smile appeared. "You were right about me. I was hiding, I was basically being stupid by letting my past screw up my future."

She raced to his arms. "I love you, too. I'm glad you finally realized that I'm not a liability."

He showered her face with kisses. "Oh, really? You haven't seen the price tag on that ring yet."

And there's more
ROSE TATTOO!

Turn the page for a bonus look at what's in store for you in the next Rose Tattoo book by Kelsey Roberts, coming to you in August 1998.

UNFORGETTABLE NIGHT

Only from Kelsey Roberts and Harlequin Intrigue!

Prologue

She opened her eyes and the first thing she noticed was the blood. The front of her dress was covered with a big stain. Instinctively, she felt her chest and stomach for wounds. That's when she felt the knife.

A misting rain began as she reached into the pocket and carefully pulled it out by the handle. There was more blood. Panicking, she tossed the knife on the ground, then wiped her hand on the hard stone behind her.

The mist was quickly turning into a heavy rain as she stood up. Shielding her eyes with her hand, she looked around. She was alone in the cemetery and that was almost as scary as seeing the blood.

When the dark cloud opened, she raced for the nearest shelter, which happened to be a mausoleum. The stain started to fade, though her anxiety was stronger than ever.

Moving to where the rain fell from the roof in a waterfall fashion, she held out her clothing and rinsed it clean, then did the same with her hands. She was soaked and cold, so she huddled in the structure, eyes wide as she read the names and dates on the vaults.

They were unfamiliar. In fact, everything was unfamiliar. Then it struck her. She knew she was fifteen. She didn't know how, she just knew it when she read the date on one of the plaques.

She also knew she was afraid, especially when she saw a figure coming toward her. A hooded slicker covered his face, and all she could think to do was be as quiet as possible.

"I thought I saw someone down here when I was driving by," he said as he pushed the hood off his head and shook off some of the rain. Water pooled at his feet, and she had a flash of seeing another pool of liquid, only it wasn't rain.

She cowered against the wall, terrified even though the elderly man was looking at her with kind eyes.

"Are you lost, honey? Where are your parents?"

She blinked, understanding the questions but unable to answer. It wasn't that she didn't want to answer. She couldn't.

"Cat got your tongue?" he asked with a smile.

"No, sir."

He lifted the poncho over his head and said, "Let's get you out of this weather. Mrs. Pendleton's is just a few miles down the road. We'll get you dry and warm until your folks come for you."

He held the slicker like a tarp and waited. "You can't stay in here, honey. You don't need to be afraid," he said as he took a step closer.

“We’ll call your folks and get you home lickety-split. I’m Joe Gomez, but most folks just call me Gomez. What’s your name?”

The blood. The knife. She must have done something terrible! “DeLancey,” she said as she read from one of the memorial plaques. “DeLancey Jones.”

She offered a weak smile as she moved toward him. He chuckled. “For a minute there I thought you’d forgotten your own name.”

She didn’t look him in the eye, because the truth was, she had.